SIGNED
SEAL'd
AND DELIVERED

JACK SILKSTONE

BOOKS

SIGNED
SEAL'd
AND DELIVERED

JACK SILKSTONE

vinci
BOOKS

This book is dedicated to the Military Working Dogs who have served, loyal and steadfast, alongside their handlers in the world's deadliest conflict zones.

Vinci Books

vinci-books.com

Published by Vinci Books Ltd in 2025

1

A CIP catalogue record for this book is available from the British Library.
Paperback ISBN: 9781036703875

The EU GPSR authorised representative is Logos Europe, 9 rue Nicolas Poussion, 17000 La Rochelle, France
contact@logoseurope.eu

By Jack Silkstone

SEAL

SEAL of Approval
SEAL the Deal
Signed SEAL'd and Delivered

Chapter One

Mike Saunders lay on a deck chair under a tree in the front yard of his house. A warm breeze rustled the leaves above as he stretched his muscled arms high and folded them behind his head. The corners of his mouth turned up in a smile and the edges of his grey eyes crinkled as he watched his son playing.

The two-year-old charged around the lawn with Axe, Mike's recently retired military working dog. The Belgian Malinois adored Junior and was closely supervising the toddler's activities.

Mike watched as Junior made a break toward his wife's rose bushes. Axe leaped into action, gently blocking his progress.

Junior clutched the dog's long fur, and the hound guided him back to the middle of the lawn. When the toddler was safe Axe sat on his haunches and looked toward Mike. One of his ears flopped over and his tongue lolled from the side of his mouth.

"Who needs a nanny when you've got Axe?" said a soft voice from behind.

He turned and watched his wife cross the lawn from the porch of their townhouse. Alison Saunders wore a floral print dress that hugged her curves, putting an even broader smile on his face.

His wife, a veterinarian, had bright green eyes, a button nose and plump lips that were perpetually turned up in a smile.

"What would we do without him?"

Ali reached the deck chair, hitched her dress and straddled him, leaning forward to kiss him. "Not as much of this."

Mike slipped his hands around her waist as she nibbled his lip. He felt the blood rush into his shorts as she ground down on him. "Spring is in the air?" he murmured.

Ali turned her attention to his ear, soft lips brushing the lobe. "It's a pity we've got an audience," she whispered.

Mike turned and looked directly into two pairs of bright inquisitive eyes. Both his son and dog were watching intently. "Isn't it time for Junior's nap?"

Ali nibbled his ear. "A huh, and if you put him to bed, we can have a nap of our own."

Mike slid his hands under her dress and along her thighs. "I'm heading out on an exercise. I'm not interested in napping."

She sat upright, shifting weight on to his crotch as she traced her fingers down his granite hard abs. "I suggest reading him *Bish the Adventure Jug*; it's his current favorite."

He groaned as she slid off him and walked toward the house. The dress did nothing to hide the lines of her butt as she climbed the porch. "Anytime now," she said with a chuckle as she disappeared inside.

Mike grinned to himself as he rose from the chair and crossed the lawn. He had to be one of the luckiest men alive, with a stunning wife, vibrant young son, great teammates and a killer job. He ruffled his dog's ears, a loyal best friend. Life was good.

Scooping his son from the grass he carried him toward the front door. As he reached for the handle, he sensed something was off and turned back to the yard.

Axe stood, staring past the rose bushes and through their white picket fence. Hackles raised and ears angled forward, it was body language that Mike knew from their time in combat.

"What's up boy?" Mike scanned the street as he bounced his son on his hip.

There were a half-dozen cars parked opposite, and he scanned each one. He spotted a white sedan in the shade of a leafy tree, and his eyes narrowed. Three years earlier, a similar car had played a role in the abduction and attempted murder of Ali. Shaking his head, he drove the idea from his mind; Barbosa was rotting in a maximum-security prison with eight life sentences.

Axe let out a half-hearted bark before joining him on the porch. The dog looked at him with intelligent brown eyes.

"What's up bud, squirrel?"

Axe cocked his head, and his right ear flopped forward. Mike reached down and ruffled his ears. Then he left the porch and walked through to Junior's bedroom. Axe's claws rattled on the floorboards as he followed. The toddler struggled to keep his eyes open as Mike tucked him into bed.

"Dadda, Axe," he managed between yawns.

"He's right here, bud." Mike kissed Junior on his forehead as the dog jumped onto the bed and curled up along-side his son.

He stroked Axe and kissed Junior again. Pausing a moment at the door, he smiled as his son reached out and placed one hand on the dog's paw. From the moment that Ali had introduced their son to his dog, the two had become inseparable. The former military working dog had taken it upon himself to watch over Junior and keep him safe.

"They're so cute," whispered his wife as she slipped an arm around his waist.

"Yeah." He turned and dipped his head to kiss her.

What started as a tender embrace rapidly escalated to heated passion as he maneuvered her into the hall. Items of clothing dropped to the floor as they continued along the passage into their bedroom. Mike removed her bra with a deft flick of his wrist and lifted her off the ground. She wrapped her legs around him as they kissed. Then he lowered her gently onto the bed.

"Can't TJ cancel the exercise so you can stay at home?" Ali purred.

Mike chuckled. "That ain't gonna happen. The old man spends all his time at the office."

"Trouble at home?"

He kissed her neck, gently brushing his lips against her skin. She moaned as he caressed her breasts. Slipping his fingers into the sides of her French cut briefs he slid them along her thighs as he continued kissing his way down her body.

Outside, less than fifty yards away in a white car, a man sat hunched over a tablet. On the seat next to him was a compact camera with a long lens.

On screen, he sorted through photos of Mike and his family as they relaxed in their yard. Selecting four images, he transferred them into an encrypted email account and hit send. Then he fished a phone from the pocket of his jacket. Holding the device to his mouth he recorded a message.

"I've sent you the pictures. Let me know what the next move is," he said in Spanish.

A moment later the message was sent and he awaited a reply. It came less than thirty seconds later in the form of text.

Maintain observation.

———

Ali took a sip from her coffee before slotting it into the cup holder on the handle of Junior's stroller. Her son was attached to his father's leg as Mike tossed a gear bag into the back of his pickup.

"Dadda, no go," he wailed.

Mike scooped him into his arms. "Hey bud, dad's got to go to work. I need you to stay here and look after mom and Axe."

"Nooo," he said shaking his head.

Ali thought her heart would break as her son buried his head into her husband's shoulder and clung to him like a koala. Feeling pressure against her leg she glanced down and saw that Axe was sitting alongside her. The dog had an uncanny knack for sensing emotions and offering support. She reached down and stroked his head.

"Hey bud, I gotta go look after my team. I'll only be gone a few days. Axe and mom need you here."

Axe barked, gaining Junior's attention, then jumped up on Mike so he could lick the boy's leg. The toddler's mood changed instantly. He giggled and reached for the dog's ears. "Dadda, down."

Mike lowered him, and he immediately wrapped his arms around Axe's neck.

"He's distracted, you need to go now," said Ali.

Mike nodded, stepped across and embraced her, kissing her softly. "I'll be back in a few days." Then he checked to make sure Axe and Junior were well clear of the pickup before jumping inside and pulling out of the drive. He gave Ali a wave as he drove away.

Once the truck had disappeared, she gathered her giggling son from the ground and placed him in the stroller. Axe stayed closed, continuing his role as the distractor.

"OK, boys. Let's get rolling."

Ali pushed the stroller across the lawn and out the gate. Axe fell in by her side. He was more than familiar with the routine of delivering Junior to daycare. The dog waited patiently as she secured the gate and handed her son a juice box. Then, with coffee in hand, they started the half-mile stroll.

For the last two months Ali had been working three half-days a week with Junior going to daycare and Axe joining her at the clinic. It was good for both of them. The toddler got to socialize, and she was able to return to the job she loved.

The walk was made even more enjoyable by the pleasure that Axe got from it. The dog's nose worked overtime as they passed houses and then shops. Ali had worried that he would miss working with Mike and the team. However, he seemed more than content in his role as Junior's guardian. He trotted alongside the stroller, sticking his head in every now and then to check on his charge.

Ali had finished her coffee when they arrived at the

daycare center. She unstrapped Junior, and he took off at lightning speed, heading straight for the jungle gym. She smiled. He was so much like his father, always charging off on another adventure.

She checked in with the staff before starting home with Axe and the stroller. The dog wore a worried expression, glancing back over his shoulder every few feet.

"It's OK, Axe. He's going to be fine."

As they moved across the parking lot Axe's attention returned to his surroundings, and Ali's thoughts turned to her day at the clinic. Today, she was expecting a broad range of patients: two Labradors, a Cocker Spaniel and a Chihuahua.

Axe interrupted her thoughts when he stopped dead and let out a low growl. Ali turned in the direction he was looking and wound his lead in a little tighter. "What is it, boy?"

There were a handful of cars in the parking lot and no pedestrians. Axe seemed to be fixated on a white sedan that had pulled in only moments earlier. The vehicle drove slowly, seemingly searching for a park. It passed two empty spots then exited onto the main road. Once it was gone Axe relaxed and sat on his haunches.

Ali knelt beside him and stroked his neck. "You didn't like that car, did you, buddy?"

He licked her cheek, and Ali chuckled. "OK, let's get to work." The rest of the walk home was uneventful, and soon they were on their way to her practice. She considered ringing Mike and telling him about the incident in the parking lot. But, she quickly pushed the idea from her mind. Axe had been through a lot in his life; he was allowed to have a little outburst every now and then.

Meanwhile, a little over twelve miles away at Halsey Field, Coronado Naval Base, Mike and his teammates, Rick and Ernie, were dressed in combat fatigues as they checked their equipment. Behind them, sailors were preparing an eleven-meter Rigid Hull Inflatable Boat (RHIB) for parachute insertion.

The SEALs had laid their gear out on the floor of a hangar so they could double-check their mission essential kit. Parachutes, wetsuits, combat harnesses, fins, radios, weapons, NVGs, batteries and helmets were inspected and accounted for.

Rick, a muscle-bound African American, checked his watch as he sipped from a can of energy drink. "Where's TJ? Not like pops to be late."

Chisel-jawed with a shaved head, Rick was the team's Corpsman. The former ladies' man had found love when Mike's bachelor party had gone badly wrong in the wilds of an Oregon forest.

"His wife was dropping him off," added Ernesto, or Ernie as his friends called him. The compact Latino was the team's comms guy and a family man with two boys.

"Deborah is going to drop him off at work?" asked Mike, as he adjusted the straps on his gear bag.

"I know, essé. Been on team with the guy for six years and I think I've met his wife twice."

"Doing better than me, I've never met her," added Rick as he finished the energy drink and crushed it.

"I met her once," said Mike.

"In my mind I picture her being statuesque," said Rick.

Mike shook his head. "Statuesque? Since when do you use words like statuesque to describe a woman?"

Rick tossed the can in the trash. "What? I just picture the Chief with someone empowered and yet elegant."

Mike and Ernie started at him in disbelief.

"There's something wrong with you." Mike finished with his gear. "I'm going to check the team rooms. The Chief might have gotten caught up."

Ernie gestured to the RHIB, where the riggers were making the final adjustments to the boat. "As soon as these guys are done we're supposed to be airborne."

Mike nodded and strode out of the hangar toward the team rooms. As he rounded the corner he spotted TJ unloading bags from a Mercedes sedan in the parking lot. A tall woman in an elegant suit stood at the driver's door of the car, Deborah.

Mike paused as TJ slung his bag over his shoulder and slammed the trunk. He watched as the veteran SEAL walked to his wife and stopped two feet from her. Mike couldn't hear what was being said, but from Deborah's body language it wasn't a fond farewell. She had her arms folded in front of her chest and was tapping her foot impatiently.

Feeling like he was intruding, Mike turned and returned to the hangar.

"You find him?" asked Ernie.

"Yeah, he's on his way."

"How's Junior and Ali doing?" asked Rick as he joined them.

"Good, bud. Junior's in daycare now and Ali's back at work."

"How's Axe handling that?"

"He's been heading to the surgery with Ali."

"I bet he's missing team life," added Ernie.

TJ appeared at the hangar entrance with his gear bag slung over his shoulder. With a square jaw and craggy features the Chief looked every bit the veteran operator that he was. A team guy through and through he'd been kicking doors and driving boats for over twenty years.

"How's it hanging, Chief?" Rick asked as TJ dumped his gear on the floor.

The squad leader fixed him with an icy stare. "What the hell is that supposed to mean?"

Rick swallowed. "Nothing, just wanted to know how you're doing."

"I'm fine. Got all your gear?"

"Team's fully accounted for," replied Ernie. "Your stuff is over next to mine."

"And the boat?"

"Riggers are finishing up now," added Mike.

"Good, soon as they're done load up and we'll get going." TJ strode across to his own equipment, leaving the boys to check on the boat.

"What the hell's wrong with him?" asked Rick in a low voice.

"He probably missed his coffee, you know how he gets," answered Ernie as he checked the shackles that attached the bundle of parachutes to the rubber boat.

"Yeah, grumpy as hell."

"Hey, how's Jenny going at her new job?" Mike said steering the conversation away from TJ.

Rick grinned. "She loves it. Very different to up north, but still plenty of critters to look after." His girlfriend was a park ranger.

"And the apartment, how you going with a woman in the house?"

He shrugged. "All good."

"All good?"

10

"OK, OK, I like it. She's great company and damn can she cook."

Mike turned to Ernie and smirked, the Latino winked and started whistling a tune. It took him a moment to realize it was Beyonce's *Single Ladies*.

"Quit grab-assing and get that damn boat loaded!" bellowed TJ from the other side of the hangar.

"Jeez, he is shitty," added Rick as he waved a cargo loader forward.

"Yeah," murmured Mike as he watched his squad leader stuff gear into a dive bag.

"Well, let's hope he chills out on the flight. Otherwise, this is going to be a long job."

Chapter Two

Vincent Barbosa sat cuffed with his hands shackled to a stainless steel table in a prison visitor's cell. The former cartel kingpin, known as *The Butcher*, wore a bright orange jumpsuit. A thick mustache adorned his face along with a smug look as he stared up at the security camera in the corner of the room.

"What's the holdup?" He shook his chains and spat into the corner.

A moment later there was a rattle from the room's steel door and it swung open, revealing a middle-aged man dressed in an ill-fitting suit, clutching a brown suitcase. Past his shoulder Barbosa caught a glimpse of a burly prison guard.

"You've got five minutes," barked the guard.

Barbosa's lawyer knew the drill. He scurried into the room and sat in the chair opposite, opening the briefcase to remove paperwork and a pen. "Sir, I've got some documents for you to sign."

"The usual?"

"Yes." He took an envelope from the case. "I also have a letter from your wife and children. I spoke to them this morning. They are well and send their love." The lawyer shot a look at the camera in the corner of the room as he slid the pen and documents across.

He took the pen and scribbled his signature in the required places.

The lawyer watched, glancing up at the camera every few seconds.

Barbosa leaned forward so he could tuck the letter from his family into the top pocket of his jumpsuit. "How is the plan progressing?"

The lawyer held up his hand as he rechecked the camera. As he did, it swiveled until the lens was facing the wall. He checked his watch. "OK, now we can talk. We've got two minutes before they start recording again."

"And?"

"Of course, the plan. Yes, it's progressing well. According to my sources, you will be transferred to another maximum security prison in Arizona."

"Do you have the date and time?"

The lawyer nodded. "Arrangements are being made."

Barbosa smiled. "Good, and what about my friends in San Diego, how are they?"

The lawyer swallowed. "My associate tells me they are in good health."

"Even the dog?"

"Yes, the dog is still with them."

His lip curled into a half snarl. "So nice to hear that nothing has happened to them."

The lawyer adjusted his tie. "Are we to proceed?"

"As planned."

"Very good." He checked the time. "There are other

matters we must discuss. One of your men is suspected of being an agent for the Sinaloa cartel."

"Who?"

"Eduardo Salcido."

Barbosa stared intently at the lawyer, who glanced up at the camera. "I never liked that worm. Have Duvan take care of him."

"Yes, sir." He checked his watch. "That's all we've got time for today."

The camera swiveled to face them.

The lawyer gathered up the papers. Then he rose and tucked his suitcase under his arm. "I'll see you soon."

Barbosa snorted. "I'll try to be here."

There was a familiar rattle, and the door opened. "You're done," ordered the guard.

Barbosa sat, quietly reflecting on the conversation as he waited for the guards to arrive and return him to his cell. Finally, after three long years, he was going to see vengeance for the wrongs against him. Finally, his brother Juan would get the justice he deserved.

A bell chimed as Ali pushed open the door to her favorite café, The Spanner Shop, a former garage that had been converted into a funky eatery. She spotted her sister, Leonie, at the rearmost table. The curvy brunette was sitting with a taller woman who had her back to the door, Jenny.

Athletic with almost jet-black hair, the park ranger had been dating Mike's teammate, Rick, ever since she and Ali had saved his SEAL team from red neck drug growers. She'd subsequently moved to San Diego and had become one of her closest friends. The three of them, Ali, her sister and Jenny met weekly for lunch or coffee at the café.

"Hey you," exclaimed Leonie as Ali took a seat.

"Hi guys."

"We've ordered you a coffee," added Jenny.

"Thanks, after this morning I need it."

"What's up?" asked Jenny.

"That gorgeous boy giving you trouble?" asked Leonie.

Ali shook her head. "Not at all. He's an angel, just like his dad. No, I had a rehabilitation session with a young Labrador. Eighty pounds of fur, tongue and slobber."

"Sounds like fun," said Jenny. "Where's Axe?"

"Christine took him for a walk," she replied, referring to her assistant at the practice.

A waiter arrived with a tray of coffees and placed them on the table.

"So, what's news with you?" Ali asked Jenny.

Jenny smirked as she reached out and grasped her coffee with her left hand. As she did Ali spotted a glint of light reflecting from a stone on her finger.

"No way," she squealed.

It took Leonie a split second to realize what was going on and add her own delighted screams to the cacophony. She leaped out of her chair and barged around the table. Stepping past her sister, she wrapped her arms around Jenny's athletic frame and almost crushed her. "Oh my god, that is so exciting. I'm so happy for you."

Ali managed to squeeze in and join the hug. "Congratulations, gorgeous."

When the excitement had subsided, Ali asked, "So, how did he do it? Give us all the details."

"Yes," added Leonie as she returned to her chair. "Every sordid morsel."

Jenny shot them a sheepish look as she sipped her coffee.

"What?" asked Ali.

"Oh god, don't tell me he tied it to his dick with a ribbon," exclaimed Leonie.

Jenny nearly spat out her coffee. "No, he certainly did not."

"Well come on then, spill the beans. How did San Diego's most eligible bachelor drop the question?"

"Well... he kind of didn't."

Ali gave her a sister a questioning look before turning to Jenny. "What do you mean?"

Jenny wore a cheeky smile. "I may or may not have asked him."

"Get out of town," bellowed Leonie.

"No way," added Ali. "And he said yes?"

Jenny nodded. "He even cried."

"That's adorable.".

"But you can't repeat that, he'd be mortified if the boys knew. I mean they're going to give him hell when they find out we're engaged."

"They don't know?" asked Ali.

She shook her head.

"Hold the farm," said Leonie. "If you proposed, where did the ring come from?"

"He already had it."

Leonie tipped her head back and laughed. "So you got the drop on Mr. Muscles. That's the best thing ever. Now, give us the deets. You take a knee and slip a ring on his finger?"

"No, I took him out to dinner and gave him a watch."

"How did you ask?" said Ali.

She shrugged. "I just asked him if he wanted to get married."

"And?"

"And then he took a knee and said yes."

"And cried!" added Leonie.

"There was a tear or two."

"That's so damn romantic... and also kind of empowering. So, when's the date?"

"July 22, we want to get married up at the cabin."

"Back where it all began," said Ali. "It seems like yesterday we were up there saving the boy's asses."

"Seems like yesterday they were putting you through that crazy selection course," added Leonie. "Which reminds me. Did Rick pass anymore of your challenges?"

Jenny shook her head. "No, he failed the Home Depot challenge with flying colors. We both got kicked out after he wore a lamp shade as a hat."

Leonie and Ali laughed.

"That's when I realized he was the one."

Mike slipped his combat rig over his head and adjusted the side straps. Then he climbed into his parachute harness and tightened it. As he did, he glanced sideways to where Rick and the others were doing the same.

The team and their gear were squeezed in alongside the RHIB that had been loaded into a C-17 transporter. A little under an hour from their target, TJ had given them the order to suit up.

Rick was struggling to get his broad shoulders into his harness. Mike shuffled over to help him. As he yanked the straps over the Corpsman's shoulders and passed him the ends, he noticed a shiny watch on Rick's wrist.

"New bling?" he yelled over the hum that filled the cargo hold.

Rick flashed a shit-eating grin. "Jenny bought it for me."

"That's a pretty expensive gift. You guys getting serious, hey?"

"Show me that thing," demanded Ernie from where he'd appeared. The Latino hadn't started rigging up yet, having checked the boat with the loadmaster. He grabbed Rick's wrist and pulled the watch up in front of his face. "Omega Seamaster; brother that's an expensive gift. That woman's put her mark on you."

Rick snatched his arm back.

"Quit screwing around, we've got forty minutes till we're on target," TJ yelled from down the line.

"What's up his ass?" mouthed Rick.

Mike shrugged and turned his attention back to his equipment.

Thirty minutes later the team stood ready for action. TJ moved along the line, checking each of them. Then, as second-in-command, it was Mike's responsibility to inspect the Chief's gear.

He stood in front of TJ as he ran through the checklist of safety and mission essential equipment. As he inspected the clips that attached the parachute to his squad leader's shoulders, he noticed a distant look in his eyes. "Chief, you OK?"

"Yeah, I'm good. We done here?"

He gave a thumbs-up and moved back in behind him. Looking forward he focused on the loadmaster.

The ramp of the C-17 lowered with a whine that was barely audible over the rush of air that whipped inside.

Mike could now see the ocean, reaching out to the horizon behind the aircraft. He checked his watch. It was 1733 hours. They were still on schedule to get the boat in the water before dark.

The helmeted loadmaster pointed at the team and held up his palm, then gestured to the boat and raised a thumb.

A red light flashed green and the loadmaster tossed a drogue chute over the ramp. It hauled a second parachute that yanked the RHIB free of the jet. Mike watched as the massive parachute blossomed above it and the aircraft banked.

It took less than four minutes for them to loop back around. In that time the loadmaster confirmed that the boat was afloat. Then, as they leveled out, the call of thirty seconds was made.

Mike shuffled forward with his equipment braced against his legs. His pulse pounded in his ears, his breathing was shallow and muscles taut. No matter how many times he jumped, it still terrified him. Previously he'd always had the comforting bulk of Axe strapped to his front. The dog had jumped with him on more than a dozen missions and it never bothered him.

The light turned green and the loadmaster gave them the chop. Mike lurched forward after the others and stepped off the ramp into the buffeting tornado of the slipstream. There was a roar and then silence as the aircraft disappeared behind him. Free-fall was short, only a few seconds. Mike activated his chute and braced for the jerk as it deployed. Then he glanced up to check the canopy before grasping the toggles and steering for clear air.

The rest of the team was also under canopy and heading toward the boat a half-mile distant. Mike aimed toward it and enjoyed the sensation of unpowered flight.

Then, as he got closer, he cut his equipment away. It dropped to the end of its tether and hit the water.

Seconds later he splashed in and cut away his parachute. Bobbing to the surface he struggled out of his harness, detached his fins from his belt, slipped them over his boots and kicked toward the boat.

When he arrived everyone was still in the water. Rick was the first to drag himself into the RHIB. He helped the others inside and like a well-oiled machine they went to work preparing to get underway.

Minutes later they were blasting over calm waters with the sun setting behind them. TJ stood at the center console, controlling the twin marine diesels that propelled the craft at breakneck speed across the ocean. Mike stood braced against the machine gun mounting in the bow, using his sleeve to wipe the spray from his Oakleys.

After a half hour of travel TJ throttled back the engines before killing them.

"This is our rally point. We wait here till dark and then head to the beach RV." He glanced at his watch. "Sunset is fifteen minutes away. Use that time to check your kit."

Rick threw out a sea anchor then he and Ernie sat in the bow going over their gear. Mike took the opportunity to move to the stern where TJ was studying a nautical chart.

"TJ, you doing OK?"

The Chief glared at him. "Why wouldn't I be?"

He shrugged. "Just asking."

TJ turned his attention back to the map.

Mike sat on the inflatable gunnels and checked the pouches on his combat rig.

"Deb wants a divorce," TJ stated.

The news hit Mike like a punch to the chest. TJ never

talked much about his home life, but when he did it was with nothing but admiration for his wife.

The Chief's brow furrowed as he continued to look at the chart. "She says we've been apart too much. Doesn't know who I am anymore."

Mike was lost for words. He'd never seen his squad leader so vulnerable. "I'm sorry to hear that," he managed. "Have you thought of taking some time off, heading somewhere to reconnect?"

TJ nodded. "Yeah, I suggested all that. Told her we could see a counselor. She said none of it would help. It's too late."

"It's never too late. You're not going to give up are you?"

TJ looked up at him with sad eyes. "Bud, I still love her as much as the day I married her, but I don't know what I can do."

Mike leaned forward and placed a hand on his friend's shoulder. "If there's anything Ali and I can do, just ask."

"Yeah, thanks bud." The veteran SEAL glanced at his watch, then over at Ernie and Rick, who were finalizing their gear in the bow. All vulnerability disappeared from his craggy features as he thumbed the engine starter. "All right, let's get this show on the road."

The figure in the white sedan had been watching the house for a little over half an hour, ensuring that nobody was home. He wasn't expecting the woman, dog or the child to be there, having tailed them to what he assumed was her sister's house across town. However, the family did have a cleaner and he didn't want her interrupting his work. It had happened on a previous job and hiding the body had proven to be a time-consuming undertaking.

Confident that the house was empty he slipped from his sedan, crossed the street and made his way along the sidewalk.

The suburb was relatively well to do and he'd tailored his disguise accordingly. He wore tracksuit pants and a San Diego Padres hoodie. He held a dog leash and had a backpack over his shoulder. It was all part of his 'Have you seen my dog?' cover story.

As he reached the target house, he glanced up and down the street. There was no one in sight, so he slipped the latch and entered the yard. Walking across the lawn he squeezed down the side of the townhouse into a tiny courtyard. The front of the home was exposed. However, a high fence and shrubs hid the rear.

A sensor light clicked on as he approached the door, slipping a lock clicker from his pocket. He smirked as he quickly picked the deadlock and pushed open the door. His employer was paying top dollar for his skills and so far it looked like a walk in the park.

The intruder knew there would be an alarm and his intuition told him exactly where the panel would be. He started a countdown in his head as he padded through a modern kitchen into a central hall. The alarm panel was on the wall a short distance from the front door. His count reached five as he examined the high-end unit. It was one he was familiar with. Popping the cover, he punched in an override code and killed a flashing red light.

Checking his watch he moved swiftly through the three-bedroom townhouse, examining each room. He paused in the doorway of what looked to be the nursery. There was a cot on one side, toy box, wardrobe and the floor was littered with plush toys. He wondered what the boy's parents had done to anger the man who'd purchased his services. Not that it mattered to him. Cash was cash. He nudged a stuffed bear with his sneaker before turning and continuing his search.

He found what he was looking for in the third bedroom. A home office had been set up at the end of the bed. A shiny aluminum laptop sat on a stand over a wireless keyboard and mouse. A touch of the keyboard brought the screen to life. The computer was locked with a password, no surprises there. He took a USB drive from his pocket and connected it.

As the software worked, he flicked through a veterinary science catalog that he found on the desk. A minute and twenty-five seconds passed before the code he'd written successfully bypassed the security of the laptop, giving him access. He wasn't there to snoop. That would come later. Selecting a file from the USB, he dragged it onto the screen and installed an application. Then, as he deleted any trace of his presence, he heard the familiar sound of a key being inserted into a lock.

Ali balanced her sleeping toddler in one arm as she turned the key to the front door. Before she could open it, Axe let out a low growl, shoved his head into the gap and forced his way inside.

"Axe, no."

It was too late. He disappeared inside, bounding down the corridor. She cursed under her breath as she stopped at the alarm panel to disarm it. A frown creased her forehead as she realized it wasn't active. Hadn't she armed it when she left the house? There was a growl from the end of the corridor and she turned to see Axe pacing the hallway, his hackles raised and tail high. She'd seen that body language before. He was hunting.

Ali's pulse quickened as she fumbled in her bag for the can of mace Mike insisted she carry.

"Axe, Axe, Axe," murmured Junior on her hip.

"Yes, buddy, it's Axe," she murmured as she flicked the safety bail off the can and moved slowly down the corridor.

The dog appeared from her study with his ears up and moved through to the kitchen. Ali followed him with the mace held ready. Axe went straight to the back door and sniffed around it while growling. A quick glance through the window didn't reveal anything out of the ordinary, so she placed the can on the bench and let him out.

Axe bolted into the yard and made for the far corner where he sniffed around in the dirt. Ali watched from the doorway as he checked every inch of the garden.

"Squirra," declared Junior as he pointed at a tree in the backyard.

Ali spotted a rodent clinging to the trunk six feet off the ground and shook her head. "Yep, it's a squirrel darling." She closed the door, leaving Axe to continue his obsession with the rodent. "OK, little man. It's time to get you to bed."

Outside on the street the intruder pulled his car over to the side of the road and took a tablet from the sports bag on the passenger seat. Opening an application he waited thirty seconds for the device to connect to the implant on his target's computer. Then he confirmed he had access to the operating system before sending a short message to his client.

I'm in.

24

Chapter Three

"Hey bro, I think we should have turned up that last valley," whispered Rick as he knelt alongside Mike.

The SEAL team was a quarter-mile from their insertion point in some of the thickest jungle they'd ever experienced. They'd only been ashore overnight, and already they were covered from head to toe in mud, sweat and slime from the river where they'd stashed the boat.

Mike took a map from a pouch on his chest rig and checked it. A moment later he confirmed Rick's doubts. "I think you're right."

The Corpsman waved a mosquito the size of a small bird away from his face. "Other people come to Hawaii to vacation," he muttered. "So, what's up with the old man? His mind ain't on the job."

Mike shrugged. "Not for me to say."

"What's not for you to say?" Ernie appeared alongside.

"Nothing," said Rick. "Just bitchin' about these damn mosquitoes."

TJ joined them. "We need to backtrack a little, but

we've got time for a short break." He slumped against a tree and took a sip from the hydration hose that hung over his shoulder.

Rick shot Mike a look before making himself comfortable next to Ernie.

Mike watched the Chief's face. Behind the thick layer of camouflage cream, he could see that his friend was hurting. He was dealing with a problem that couldn't be solved with tactical maneuver and firepower.

"I think we need to talk about the elephant in the room," said Ernie between bites of an energy bar.

TJ's eyes narrowed as he turned to Mike. "What elephant is that?"

"Rick's engagement watch."

Mike and TJ both turned to face the Corpsman.

"Engagement watch, is that even a thing?" asked Mike.

"Why else would she buy him a sweet-ass watch?" said Ernie.

TJ looked relieved that the attention was away from him. "Seems legit. So, what's the go Romeo? That woman of yours laid claim?"

Mike couldn't remember the last time he'd seen Rick embarrassed. The Corpsman fiddled with the sight on his assault rifle and avoided eye contact.

"Holy crap, it's true," said Mike.

Rick sighed. "Yeah it's true. We're engaged. She got a ring and I got a watch."

"Bro, that's awesome news," said Mike.

Ernie slapped his teammate on the shoulder. "Congratulations, essé. I guess this means you passed her selection."

"Good work, son," added TJ.

Rick smiled sheepishly. "So, you're not going to give me shit?"

"About what?" asked Mike. "This is great news."

"About the watch?" Rick replied.

"What about it? I mean it's a really good-looking watch. Has to be worth a few dollars?" said Mike.

"Come on guys, quit messing with me."

The three men stared at him blankly.

"The watch?" said Rick. "Ernie literally told you what it was."

The Latino shrugged. "An engagement watch?"

Suddenly, Mike got what he was saying. "Holy shit, she proposed to you, didn't she?"

Rick nodded sheepishly.

"Shit essé, that's straight up brutal. Did she drop to a knee?" added Ernie.

"OK, enough," grumbled TJ. "We've got a mission to roll." He rose, prompting the other men to do the same.

Mike offered Rick a hand and hauled him from the ground.

"What's up with the Chief, man? He didn't bat an eyelid when he found out. In fact, he looked sad as hell," murmured Rick.

"He's got a lot going on."

"You don't say."

Rick started off after TJ while Mike waited to take his position at the rear. As they slid down a steep slope, back toward the river, he found himself thinking about the amount of time he spent away from Ali and Junior. If time away was what broke TJ's relationship then he was going to have to get better at work-life balance.

Mike and the rest of the team sat in thick jungle on the slope of a long-dead volcano as a pair of F/A-18 Hornets screamed up the valley. He watched through binoculars as each jet released two bombs before shooting near vertical into the sky.

Flashes and billowing balls of dust and debris marked the impact of the bombs on target three seconds before the sound of the explosion reached them. "Target destroyed."

Ernie repeated the confirmation into the radio, informing headquarters that the mission had been completed.

"Job well done," announced TJ as they packed up their gear.

"Evac bird is inbound to the LZ," added Ernie.

The four men finished stowing their equipment and hiked the final quarter-mile to a clearing at the lip of the former volcano. On arriving they dropped their packs and waited for the helicopter.

"This place isn't so bad when you're not slugging it out with the jungle," said Rick as they admired the view out over the training area to the ocean. The four men sat in silence, enjoying the serenity of the morning.

"I let you guys down today," TJ said breaking the silence. "My mind hasn't been on the job."

"We all have our off days, Chief," said Rick.

"Yeah, remember that time I forgot the radio batteries," added Ernie.

"You wanna talk about it?" asked Rick.

Mike caught the Corpsman's eye and shook his head. The last thing TJ would want was to share his problems with everyone else. He was amazed the Chief had even told him.

"Deb wants a divorce," said TJ, matter of fact.

The team was silent.

"I'm sorry to hear that, Chief," said Rick as the beat of a helicopter's blades reached their ears.

"No, I'm sorry for putting a dampener on your news."

"I think we all need a beer," said Mike as their ride thundered overhead.

"I know a good steakhouse in Honolulu," added Ernie as they gathered their gear. "When's our flight home?"

"Tomorrow at 0930," replied Mike.

"Chopper's going to drop us at the boat. We should be back in Pearl by lunchtime and wrapped up by 1600," said TJ.

"Then beer and steak it is," said Ernie.

———

A few hours later on the other side of the Pacific Ali had walked Axe to the daycare facility to pick up Junior. As she fastened him in his stroller for the walk home, her phone rang. She took it from her pocket and checked the screen. It was Mike. "Hey handsome, can you give me a few seconds?" Attaching a pair of buds and slipping them into her ears she took her place behind the stroller. "Hey, I'm back. What's up? How did the exercise go?" She began walking with Axe alongside the stroller.

"It was good, we're all done now. I just wanted to call and tell you and Junior that I love you both."

"And we love you. Are you still back tomorrow?"

"Yeah, can't wait to see you."

Ali thought she could detect something in Mike's voice. "Babe, is everything OK?"

There was a pause. "Yeah, I just wanted you to know

how much I love you and appreciate the hard work you put in."

Ali frowned. "Thanks, babe… Are you sure everything is OK?"

There was a pause.

"Deborah wants a divorce. TJ's not taking it well."

"I'm sorry to hear that. Is there anything I can do?"

"No, we're heading out to dinner now. Hopefully, he'll open up a little over a few beers."

"Mike, I know you mean well, but sometimes people need a little space to work out their problems. I don't want you guys coming up with a harebrained scheme to try and help."

"When has that ever happened?"

"When has it ever not?"

There was a pause. "Good point. We'll keep it low key."

"Good idea. OK, love you handsome. I'll see you tomorrow."

"Love you too."

Ali ended the call as they reached the street before their block. While she checked for traffic, she found herself thinking about TJ and Deborah. She'd only met her a few times, but Deb was always lovely. What's more, TJ had made her feel like part of the team. He was the wise sage that she could turn to for advice on anything. It saddened her to think of how much pain he must be dealing with.

A loud bark from Axe drew her attention and she glanced across the street in the direction he was looking. There were some cars parked by the side of the road. She stopped and ruffled Axe's ears. "What's up, bud?"

The dog growled.

Ali checked across the street and spotted a figure sitting in a white sedan. "It's OK Axe."

Something about the car had spooked the dog and it left her feeling uneasy.

She returned to behind the stroller and pushed it quickly along the sidewalk. Axe fell into place but kept glancing across at the car.

As they progressed the dog seemed to calm. By the time they reached their townhouse he was a little less agitated. He stood watch by the front door as she opened it and bundled Junior inside. Her son was asleep, exhausted from daycare. She called Axe inside and locked the door.

Moving into the sitting room, she left Junior sleeping in his stroller. Axe was by her side as she peered through the blinds. A moment later her concerns were confirmed. The white car drove slowly past the house.

Ali checked on Junior as she took her phone from the stroller. Her finger hovered over the button to call Mike. Was she being paranoid? She decided against ringing him and stepped away from the window, glancing down at Axe. They were more than capable of looking after things until Mike got home tomorrow. In the meantime, she needed to get Junior fed and into bed before checking her emails.

Mike raised a beer-filled glass in the air and cleared his throat. "To Jenny and Rick."

The other members of the team followed suit, raising their drinks and echoing the words over the background noise of the bar. They'd followed Ernie's advice and ended up in a steakhouse called the Yard House. With over a hundred beers on tap, it was a perfect fit for the thirsty SEAL team.

"If I can give you one tip," added TJ. "Make Jenny the

most important thing in your world. The teams will come and go. You're marrying her for life."

Mike could see the pain in TJ's eyes as he delivered his heart-felt advice.

Rick nodded solemnly.

"Shouldn't be a problem," added Ernie, with a wink. "She already wears the pants."

Rick shook his head as the others broke into laughter.

A waitress appeared and TJ ordered another round. "Thanks, guys. I needed this."

"That's what we're here for," said Mike.

"Yeah, although I'm not usually the one needing advice."

"No, that's true. It always used to be Mike and his latest girlfriend problems, or Rick and his latest STD," said Ernie.

There was more laughter.

"Oh, it's pick on Rick day is it?"

"Just wait for the bachelor party," said Ernie. "It's payback time."

The waitress returned with their beers.

"In all seriousness, though," TJ continued, "I don't know what to do. Deb won't consider seeing a counselor. She says it's too late. It's over."

All three men could see the pain on their squad leader's face.

"SEALs don't give in that easy, Chief," said Mike. "If you love her, you need to fight for her."

"Yeah," echoed Ernie. "And if we can do anything to help, just ask."

TJ nodded. "You can start by joining me in another toast." He gestured for the waiter. "Can we get five tequilas, please."

"Five?" enquired Mike.

TJ shot him a sly grin. "Two for Rick."

"Damn straight."

Rick slapped his palm on the table. "Hell, yeah. Let's get this party started."

Mike shook his head. It was going to be one of those nights.

Chapter Four

Ali handed Junior a piece of brown toast smothered in avocado and smiled as he attacked it with gusto. Her son had yet to master eating rather than wearing his food. As he continued to smear himself she walked through the house and glanced out the front window. Axe followed her and stood at the door.

There was no sign of the car from last night. She glanced at the dog and noticed that he was completely relaxed. If Axe didn't sense a threat then she had nothing to fear. A former SEAL working dog, he was the best body-guard that she and Junior could have. Although it would be nice when Mike was back. Checking her watch she calcu-lated the time difference between San Diego and Hawaii; he would land in the next few hours.

A delighted squeal sounded from the kitchen and she checked on Junior. As predicted, he'd smeared most of his avocado across his face. Seeing he was preoccupied she ducked into the home office to check her emails. First message in the inbox was an appointment reminder. "Oh, crap." Junior was due for a checkup with the GP that morning.

Dashing into the kitchen she pried the excited toddler from his high chair, stripped him and ran him through the shower. Fifteen minutes later she had him in clean clothes and was strapping him into the booster seat in the back of her Prius.

As she closed the door Axe touched the back of her hand with his nose. She stooped to grasp his head in her hands and kiss the top of his head. "I'm sorry, bud. I can't take you to the doctor. Guard the house, we'll be back soon and so will Mike."

Axe let out a soft bark at the sound of his master's name. Then he turned and trotted across to the shade of a large tree where he sat watching Ali climb into the car. She gave him a wave, backed out onto the street and hit close on the gate remote.

As she drove she glanced in the mirror and caught Junior's reflection.

"Axe, Axe, Axe," the boy demanded.

She smiled and shook her head as he continued chanting the dog's name. In the last few months the two had become inseparable. She'd worried how Axe would deal with retirement from the SEAL team; but he'd taken to his new role like a fish to water.

As Ali's silver hybrid turned out of the street a set of eyes followed it. The man who'd broken into their home thumbed a message into his phone from where he sat in a rented yellow hatch and hit send. Then he pulled out from the curb and commenced tailing the Prius. His target had left the dog at home, making it the perfect opportunity to strike. Now, he just needed to wait for the go ahead from his client.

Barbosa lay on his bunk staring at the concrete ceiling of his cell. He knew every crease, every one of the dimples caused by air bubbles when the slab had been laid. For three years it had been the first thing and last thing he saw. Day after day, week after week, month after month, but not for much longer. A smirk formed on his lips as he imagined his return to Mexico. Yes, he would see his family, but more importantly, he would taste revenge.

A faint buzz sounded from beneath his pillow. He lifted his head and recovered his contraband cell phone. The obsolete Nokia had cost him more than a small car on the outside.

He checked the screen and smiled. There was a coded message from one of his most trusted men. He thumbed a response and waited for the confirmation. It came a moment later. The plan was in motion.

Slipping the phone beneath his pillow he sat on the edge of his bed and reached under for a small box. The battered container held the only personal items he was permitted to have in prison. He rummaged through the contents until he found the thing he was looking for. It was a photo of two men standing shoulder-to-shoulder with broad smiles on their faces. One of them was Barbosa, albeit much plumper. The other was his brother, Juan.

A vein in the side of his head pulsed as he remembered the night that an American SEAL team had come for him. He recalled, in vivid detail, the face of the man who'd fired the bullet that had killed his only brother. Mike Saunders' grey eyes and square jaw were etched into his mind.

"I will avenge you," he whispered then returned the photo to the box. He'd been planning this operation for three years, and today, it was finally going to be put into action. Mike Saunders was going to feel loss like nothing he could ever imagine.

———————

A green van, with the words Royal Garden Services stenciled on the side, turned into the Saunders' street and cruised slowly past the houses. Inside, two men dressed in grey coveralls scanned the street numbers.

"This is it," said Hugo from the passenger seat. He was the taller of the two, broad-shouldered and in his mid-twenties.

His partner Antonio, at least ten years older and thirty pounds heavier, dipped his multiple chins in concurrence. "I'll park out front." He maneuvered the van with skill, parallel parking it directly in front of the picket fence that bordered the quaint home.

Hugo jumped out of the van and opened the side door. It was empty except for a large metal crate and plastic box. As his partner joined him, he took a paper-wrapped parcel from the box. Unrolling it he revealed a juicy pink fillet steak.

"You put enough on it?" asked Antonio.

"Yeah, enough to drop a dinosaur."

"It better not kill the damn thing. I don't want a repeat of that incident in Tijuana."

"That wasn't my fault. How was I to know the old lady was already jacked up on happy pills?"

"Just get on with it."

The two men stepped away from the van and approached the fence. They were an arm's length away when a loud bark startled them both.

37

"Good doggie," murmured Hugo as he flicked the steak into the yard. The Malinois launched itself against the fence and bared a jagged set of teeth as it growled.

"Holy shit," yelled Hugo as he backpedaled.

Antonio laughed. "Hombre, it's just a dog."

"It's a monster."

"Yeah, and soon he's going to be a sleepy monster."

The men returned to the van's cabin and closed the doors. From their elevated position they could see into the yard. They watched as the dog sniffed the steak.

"Yum, yum, eat it all up," said Antonio.

Behind the fence the dog gave the steak another sniff then moved to the porch where he had better observation across his domain.

The men watched for another fifteen minutes and yet still the Malinois ignored the meat.

"Eat the steak you bastard," said Hugo.

"He will," replied Antonio.

"Maybe it's not hungry?"

"Dogs are always hungry."

"You're always hungry. That's why you're so fat."

Hugo's phone vibrated. He pulled it from the center console and inspected the screen. "We need to move now. The woman's coming back to the house."

"We'll use the dart guns."

They alighted from the van and opened the side door. From inside the box they recovered two sleek black dart guns. Both men checked the weapons were loaded. Then Hugo made for the picket gate as Antonio stepped up to the fence.

"Where is it?" asked Hugo as he leaned over the gate.

"It was on the porch."

He scanned the yard but saw no sign of the dog. "You're

kidding me." He reached over the gate and grasped the latch.

There was a savage growl and he screamed as strong jaws clamped on to his arm. Jagged teeth pierced his flesh as he wailed, "Help me, help me."

Antonio lurched forward, leaned over the fence and fired the gun. The dart shot past the dog, thudding into the lawn.

At the same time, Hugo managed to fire his weapon with his free hand. The dart lodged in the dog's shoulder but the animal growled louder, savaging his arm with a vicious shake.

"Shoot it again! Shoot it again!" Hugo screamed hysterically, bracing against the gate.

Antonio fumbled with his dart gun. Seconds passed before he reloaded, aimed and fired. The projectile flew straight and true, striking the dog in the flank. However, the two doses of sedative made no difference.

"Get him off me!" yelled Hugo as Antonio reloaded and fired yet another dart into the animal.

Finally, the attack dog released Hugo and fell back. He swayed and stumbled as he retreated to the porch.

"When he drops, you get him," said Hugo as he clutched his bloodied arm to his chest.

Antonio's eyes were wide. "I'm not going in there till he's out for the count."

Hugo found a sweater from inside the van and wrapped it around his arm to staunch the bleeding. It felt like the dog's teeth had reached the bone. "Just get the bastard dog. We need to get the hell out of here."

Junior was singing as Ali turned her Prius into their street. He had passed his checkup with flying colors. Mike was going to beam with pride when she passed on the news that he was significantly larger than other children his age.

The smile dropped from her face as Ali caught a glimpse of a man bundling a dark object into a van immediately in front of their house. The vehicle pulled away from the curb as she reached their drive. A glance out the window confirmed her worst fear. The white picket gate was smeared with blood and wide open. She jumped from the car. "Axe, Axe!" she screamed.

There was no sign of the dog.

Ali dove back into the Prius and stomped the accelerator to the floor. The little hybrid's tires chirped as it lurched forward. She aimed it down the street after the van that was turning the corner.

Her heart lurched as she lost sight of the vehicle and she urged the hybrid on. Behind her Junior squealed with delight as they zoomed around the corner, narrowly missing another car.

She'd closed the gap with the van to the point where she could read the plate number. Committing it to memory, she backed off the throttle. Mike had taught her the basics of tailing another car on one of their many road trips; one of the perks of having a SEAL as a husband.

As she drove she activated the car's entertainment system. "Dial 911," she ordered the voice recognition program.

A moment later the call connected. "Hello, you've reached 911 how may I help you?"

"Hi, look someone has abducted my dog. I'm in pursuit of a white van with the following plate number." She positioned the car so she could read off the license plate.

"Ma'am, are you in any way in danger?"

Ali shook her head. "No, someone has stolen my dog."

"Yes, ma'am I am aware and I have reported the incident. However, I need to know if your life or anyone else's life is in immediate danger."

"Yes, my dog's life is in danger."

"Understood ma'am. Officers will investigate the theft as soon as possible."

"I'm following them right now."

"Miss, that's not advised. You need to leave this to the professionals. I'll have officers get in contact with you as soon as possible."

"So that's it?" Ali thumped the steering wheel in frustration.

"Yes, ma'am. A BOLO will be issued for the van and officers will respond as quickly as they can."

Ahead Ali saw the van slow and indicate to turn left. At the same time, a pickup moved into the gap between them. If she wasn't careful, she was going to lose them.

"Ma'am is that all?"

"Huh? Yeah, that's all. Thanks for your help." She terminated the call and braked as the pickup slowed. "Get out of the way, idiot!"

"Idiot!" echoed Junior from the backseat.

"We don't say that, darling."

The pickup came to a complete stop, leaving a small gap that allowed her to squeeze around the corner. Accelerating she searched for the van. The street was empty and her heart skipped a beat. Then, she caught a glimpse of it on a side street. Slowing she turned across the opposite lane. A truck skidded to a halt, its horn blaring.

Ali whipped the hybrid into a tight U-turn and continued her chase. Further ahead the van was gathering speed. Traffic was heavier here and there was a danger that she'd lose Axe's dognappers in the afternoon rush.

A traffic signal changed to yellow as the van rushed through it. Ali gunned the engine. The light went red as the Prius belted forward. At that moment Ali realized the risks she was taking with Junior in the car. She slammed on the brakes, and the car shuddered to a halt a yard past the intersection. Ali's eyes never left the van as it escaped into traffic. Faintly, she registered the flash of movement to her right. Then there was an almighty bang as a car smashed into the Prius, flinging it sideways.

Chapter Five

Mike burst into the police station and stormed up to the counter. "I'm here to see my wife, Alison Saunders."

The elderly sergeant behind the counter looked up from his computer screen and gave the SEAL a once over. As he did, another man appeared at the door, TJ.

"Mr. Saunders, your wife and son are safe and sound in interview room one. I'll buzz you through."

As promised, Mike found Ali and Junior in an interview room with a female police officer. His wife leaped out of her chair and wrapped her arms around him. "Mike, they took Axe. I'm so sorry I couldn't stop them."

"Babe, it's OK. You and Junior are safe, that's what's important."

"You have to find him."

"Sir," said the police officer. "We've issued a BOLO on the vehicle. Our people are actively searching for your dog."

Mike nodded. "Thanks officer. Do you mind if I take my family home now?"

"No problem. We're all done here."

Mike picked up Junior and the three of them walked out to the reception area where TJ was talking with the sergeant. A moment later the Chief joined them in the parking lot.

"Cops ran the plates on the van and got nothing."

"What about the company name, Royal Garden Services?" asked Ali.

"Company's got a website, but it's not registered."

"It's a front?" asked Mike.

"Looks that way," said TJ.

"Why would someone target Axe?" asked Ali.

Mike and TJ shared a look.

"No, he's in jail. Barbosa can't possibly have done it."

"They'll try to get Axe across the border. We need to stake out the crossing points," said Mike.

"I'll get Ernie, Rick and some of the boys to help us out." TJ took his phone from his pocket and started dialing.

"Mike, what can I do?" asked Ali.

"Babe, you've done enough. If it weren't for you, we wouldn't have a lead. TJ and I will get Axe back."

"Axe, Axe, Axe!" yelled Junior.

Ali looked up at her husband with tear filled eyes. "You have to get him back."

The Royal Garden Services van pulled into a rented warehouse and a sliding door clanged shut behind it. Hugo jumped from the cabin as the lights flickered on. He spotted their employer standing alongside a stack of barrels.

"Any problems?" asked the man who'd broken into Ali and Mike's home.

"All good, essé," replied Hugo.

"All good?" squawked Antonio as he climbed from the passenger seat, clutching his bloodied arm. "That dog is loco."

The man nodded. "I told you he was an attack dog. Why did you get so close?" He spat on the floor. "Actually, I don't care. Is it sedated?"

"Yes, we dosed him good."

"He better be alive."

"He is, we're not complete amateurs."

The man raised his eyebrows as he glanced at Antonio's arm. "If you say so." Then he gestured to a flatbed truck parked on the far side of the warehouse. The tray was stacked high with blue barrels. "Put the dog in a barrel and hit the road. The quicker we get you across the border, the better."

Hugo nodded and slid the door to the van open.

"We're going to need more money," said Antonio.

"Because you screwed up?"

"No, because the dog's loco."

The burglar shook his head. "You know who's paying the bills?"

"Do I care? Look at my arm."

"You know who the Butcher is?"

The color drained from Antonio's face.

"Yeah, I thought so. Now get the dog in a barrel."

———

Mike and TJ sat in the US Customs and Border Protection command post, staring at a wall of screens. TJ had called in a favor with an FBI colleague to get them access. When he'd explained the situation to the Border Guards, they'd been only too happy to help.

"We're chasing a needle in a haystack," said Mike.

"We've got Rick and Ernie at the other checkpoints," replied TJ.

On screen, Mike watched a large flatbed truck loaded with barrels passing through one of the checkpoints. "They could have changed vehicles a dozen times by now."

TJ nodded. "Mike, we need to start thinking about enacting a contingency plan."

"The priority is Axe."

"No, the priority is keeping you and your family safe. Barbosa knows where you live."

"He's always known where we live."

"Yes, but now he's taken action on that."

"You're right, we need to confront him."

"You sure you want to do that?"

Mike turned to the Chief with a look of anguish on his face. "Do we have any other choice?"

"If he took Axe it's because he wants to bargain, and you know the only thing he wants more than that dog is you."

"Yeah, but we're not gonna let that happen."

"I'll make the arrangements."

Mike continued to watch the flow of vehicles as TJ made a call. He and Axe had served together in Afghanistan, Mexico and Columbia. The dog had saved his life and the lives of his teammates on more than one occasion. Axe had also brought Ali and him together, and saved her life. There was no way in hell that Mike was going to rest until that dog was safe at home where he belonged.

The truck ground its way along a sandy track bordered on both sides by thick scrubby bush. Hugo and Antonio had driven their cargo down the Baja peninsula to the resort town of Cabo San Lucas before heading inland. Their destination was a shabby looking ranch nestled in the foothills of a steep mountain range.

"What a dump," said Antonio as the truck's brakes hissed, sending up a cloud of yellow dust.

Las Polvo had once been a horse ranch. Now it was a dilapidated collection of adobe buildings clustered around an open square. At one end a set of yards filled with tumbleweeds was slowly disintegrating in the harsh Mexican sun.

As Hugo stepped from the truck the front door of one of the buildings opened and a figure dressed in faded jeans, boots, a check shirt and a Stetson appeared. The dog snatcher noted the Glock pistol and spare magazines attached to the man's belt, and the submachine gun slung over his shoulder. The guy looked cartel, through and through.

"You guys made good time," said the man as a second, similarly equipped *sicario* wearing a baseball cap joined him.

"Traffic was light," said Hugo.

Antonio joined them and the men eyeballed the bloodied bandaged wrapped around his arm.

The man spat tobacco into the dust. "OK essé, where's the dog?"

Hugo moved to the side of the truck and released a strap. Grasping a barrel, he hefted it clear. As he dropped it to the ground a savage growl emanated from inside.

"Angry little bastard," said one of the men.

Antonio raised his injured arm. "You could say that."

"The pens are around the back."

The cartel guy's offsider appeared with a sack truck and kicked it under the barrel. The growling continued as Hugo wheeled it behind the buildings to where there were four concrete floored pens.

Dog fighting was popular in Mexico and Hugo knew that the cartels controlled it. This must be one of the facilities where they held the dogs before the fights. As he pushed the drum into a pen he noted bloodstains on the floor, and scratch marks on the steel posts.

"Put it in the middle and undo the lid," said the *sicario*.

Hugo dumped the barrel and stepped away from it. "You do it." He left the cage.

"Pussies." The other man stepped forward and unlatched the lid. As he levered it free the dog broke into a volley of savage barks. He flipped the lid, backpedaled out of the cage and slammed the gate.

The Stetson-wearer grabbed a pole from where it leaned against the cage. Pushing it through the wire fence he gave the barrel a shove. The dog growled as it rocked. He gave it a harder shove and it toppled over.

A moment later their captive appeared, baring its teeth at the men with raised hackles.

"Shit, that's a mean looking *perro*."

Stetson handed the pole to his partner and took a phone from his pocket. "Give him a poke." He started filming as the other man shoved the pole through the fence at the dog.

Axe savaged the end of the stick, tearing it from his hands.

"He's a real feisty one. Pity the boss has got other plans for him. He'd make us a fortune in the fights."

The dog retreated to the corner with the stick and proceeded to tear it to pieces. Stetson finished filming and placed his phone in his pocket. There was no reception at the ranch. He'd head into town to upload the video.

"Have you got our money?" asked Antonio.

"Inside." He gestured for his partner to get it.

"Do you know what the plan is for the dog?" continued Antonio as they walked back to the truck.

"Oh, that hound's gonna wish he was never born."

"Good." He gestured to his bandaged arm. "Make sure he really suffers."

Chapter Six

TJ grasped Mike by the shoulder as he made to enter the visitor's cell in the Supermax prison. "Hey, don't let your emotions get the better of you in there. Remember, Barbosa is a full-blown psycho and you punched his brother's ticket. He's out for revenge and getting angry is going to play straight into his hands."

Mike nodded. "Yeah, got it."

A burly looking guard opened the door and gestured for the men to enter.

Barbosa, *The Butcher*, sat shackled to a steel table. Mike paused in the doorway. If it weren't for the eyes, he would have sworn it was a different man. Prison life had been good for the former cartel kingpin. He'd lost at least thirty pounds of fat and gained some muscle in his chest and shoulders.

"Petty Officer Mike Saunders." Barbosa greeted him with a broad smile. "It's a real pleasure to see you."

"I'm sure it is," snapped Mike as he moved inside and TJ followed him.

There was a moment of awkward silence as the three men eyeballed each other.

"So, to what do I owe the pleasure, amigos?"

"Where the hell is Axe?"

Barbosa feigned confusion. "How would I know where your tomahawk is?"

"You know exactly what I'm talking about."

"Do I?"

"My dog, where is my dog?" growled Mike.

"Easy," said TJ.

The cartel boss shrugged. "I've got no idea what you're talking about."

Mike clenched his jaw so hard his teeth hurt. He imagined reaching across, grasping Barbosa's head and smashing his face into the table.

Barbosa smiled. "How's the family, Mike? Alison and the little boy, Junior, right? It must be so nice to be able to spend time with them. Family is so important, don't you agree?"

He stepped forward. "I'm going to kill you. Just like I killed your worthless brother."

The smile dropped from Barbosa's face and for a split second Mike thought he had gotten to him. However, rage was soon replaced by a smirk. "Have fun searching for your dog."

"If you tell me where he is, I'll make it quick."

"OK, we're done here," said TJ. He turned to the camera in the corner of the room. "Guard!"

"I'm sorry, TJ," Mike said as they climbed into his truck having left the prison. "That bastard got the better of me."

"Understandable."

As Mike exhaled and inserted his key in the ignition his

phone vibrated. He took it from the center console and examined the screen.

"What is it?" asked TJ.

"A blocked number just sent me a video. It's downloading."

Mike's heart shuddered when the video started playing and he recognized Axe savaging a broom handle behind a mesh fence. He watched the short clip twice then passed it to TJ.

"At least we know he's alive," said the Chief.

Tears formed in Mike's eyes and he clenched his fists as he visualized Axe being tortured by Barbosa's men. "I need to go back in there and beat it out of him."

"Bud, he's not going to tell you. But, if we get this video to the right people, they might be able to give us a lead."

"Your guys in the FBI?"

"No. I think we need a little more clout."

Deborah Lines sat in an expensive leather chair behind a glass desk in her corner office at Style Cuisine Magazine. The statuesque brunette wore an immaculately tailored two-piece suit, white blouse and had designer glasses perched on her pointed nose.

Rocking back in her chair she tapped the glass with a Mont Blanc pen as she read a report on her Apple laptop. According to one of the Agency's analysts, there was a vigilante organization actively targeting criminals and despots with impunity across the globe. It all sounded a little fanciful to her. However, the reason the document caught her attention was that it named a former work colleague of hers as one of the organization's founders.

Vance and she had been close friends when they'd started out in the Agency. However, they had lost touch and he'd reportedly been killed in a terrorist attack in the UAE in 2003.

Her thoughts were interrupted when her cell phone vibrated. She picked it up and saw that it was a message from her recently separated husband, TJ.

"What does he want?" she mumbled as she opened the message and read the brief paragraph. Then she tapped the attached file and watched the short video.

"Son of a bitch."

Storming out of her office she weaved her way through an open plan workspace until she reached a door marked Archives. A thumb scanner gave her access to an airlock where a second device checked her retina. Finally, a door opened giving her access to a space the size of a small bedroom packed with screens and pieces of high-tech looking equipment.

"Deb, how are you?" asked one of the four people sitting at workstations in the room, a middle-aged woman with blonde bangs.

"I'm good, Lu. Look, I just emailed you a file. Can you bring it up?"

"No problems." Her fingers danced on the keys and the video TJ had sent appeared on screen. "What is this?"

"This, this is your priority. I want everything you can get me from this video."

"This got anything to do with TJ?"

Deb nodded. "Yeah, that's the dog from his team."

"The hero matchmaker?"

"The one and only. Allegedly he's been abducted and this is the only lead that TJ and his guys have."

"Ah, huh." Lu had already loaded the file into three

different programs and had set a bank of supercomputers to work. "So, how are things going with TJ?"

"He's moved out."

"So, not well."

She sighed. "In the last five years we've spent next to no time together. I barely know the guy anymore. How long do you need to work this video?"

"Give me an hour."

"I'll be in my office."

Moments later Deb was sitting back at her desk gazing at a photo she'd taken from the bottom of her filing cabinet. It was a picture of her and TJ on a beach in Mexico. The ruggedly handsome SEAL operator had his arm around her waist and they both wore broad smiles; a happier time. Sighing she returned the photo to the cabinet and turned back to her computer. She'd help TJ find Axe and then she'd need to break off all contact.

Chapter Seven

TJ pushed open the door to the café and spotted Mike, Ali and Junior sitting in the far corner. The SEAL and his wife looked like they hadn't slept. He knew how that felt. He'd been up all night contacting buddies in the FBI, DEA and every other three-letter agency, trying to get some assistance in locating Axe.

"Morning, guys." He sat at the end of the bench seat next to Ali.

Almost immediately a waiter appeared with a coffee. "A triple espresso Americano!"

He shot Mike a nod of appreciation and took a sip. "OK, guys. I've got good news and bad news. My contact managed to rip some information out of the video Mike was sent."

"Do you know where he is?" asked Mike.

"We know the broad area where the video was uploaded."

"And?"

"It was down in Mexico on the Baja peninsula near Cabo San Lucas."

"Barbosa," growled Mike.

"TJ, is there any way we can get a government agency to help?" asked Ali.

"No one's going to stick their neck out for a dog."

"Even a decorated war hero?"

He shook his head.

"Momma, where Axe?" asked Junior from where he was sitting next to Mike.

TJ's heart lurched when he saw the look of concern on the boy's face.

"We could head down there and take a look around," said Mike, his voice cracking.

"Mike, you'd be playing right into Barbosa's hands."

"I can't just give up on him."

He faintly registered the jingle of the door behind him. The expression on Mike's face told him someone he recognized had entered the café.

"Ali, Mike, good morning."

TJ turned to face his estranged wife.

She smiled politely. "Terrance, do you mind if I join you?"

"By all means."

Deb sat and gestured for the waiter. "I hope you don't mind, TJ sent me the video of Axe. I had my people work on it." She ordered a latté.

"Your people?" Ali wore a confused look. "I thought you worked for a culinary magazine?"

"We have diverse interests. The bottom line is we managed to identify the device that recorded the video."

Mike nodded. "Yeah, TJ said. Axe is in Cabo, I'm going to head down and find him."

"Mike, that's not a good idea. The cartels have a strong presence down there. A military guy sniffing around is only going to draw heat."

"Look, Axe has saved me, Ali and TJ more than once. We can't hang him out to dry."

Deb nodded. "I get that, but you need to understand the risk."

"This lead's already 24 hours old. The risk is if we don't move now we'll lose him forever."

Deb's coffee arrived and she sipped it. Once the waiter had departed she turned to TJ. "What do you think?"

TJ locked eyes with Mike. "Axe is a member of my team. If Mike goes down there I'm going with him."

"I thought as much." She took another sip. "I'll make the necessary arrangements for equipment and accommodation. It's going to look strange if I head down with the boys." She paused. "Ali, how do you feel about joining us? With you we can pass for two couples on a holiday. It would go a long way to reducing our risk profile."

Mike shot his wife a concerned look.

Ali exhaled. "I can do that."

"Who will look after Junior?" asked Mike.

"Rick and Jenny," replied Ali. "You know how clucky she's been recently. Plus, it will only be for a few days right?"

"If we move fast," said Deb.

"Then we better get organized," said Mike.

"Give me a few hours to get some equipment together and then we'll meet at yours," said Deb as they bundled Junior into his stroller.

"This means the world to us guys," said Mike as they departed.

Deb finished her coffee and made to leave. She took two paces toward the door before turning back. "Terrance, don't get any funny ideas. I'm doing this for Ali, Mike and Junior."

He nodded. "Got it."

She left and TJ sat finishing his coffee. A plan was already forming in his head as to how they were going locate Axe. They'd need to set up a surveillance net and sweep the town with specialist equipment. Having Deb on board was going to make the job a hell of a lot easier. His thoughts wandered from the pending mission to his now estranged wife. They'd never worked together before. Maybe this was the opportunity they needed to reconnect. As quickly as the thought emerged he banished it from his mind and downed the last of his coffee. The mission was recovering Axe, and that was precisely what he was going to do.

———

The look of horror on Rick's face confirmed that he was terrified of the idea of babysitting Junior. "Can't I go to Mexico?" he asked.

Mike and Ali had driven their son around to his godparent's house as part of their preparation for the mission to rescue Axe.

"No you can't," said Jenny. "Remember when we agreed to be his guardians?" She arched an eyebrow. "That comes with certain responsibilities. You need to man up." Her voice softened. "Plus, think of it as a dress rehearsal."

"Dress rehearsal for what?"

Mike, Ali and Jenny all stared at him.

"Wait, Jenny, you're not…"

His fiancée shook her head. "No, you dolt. But, we did talk about having kids soon."

"Oh yeah, right." Rick shot Mike a look of relief. "In all seriousness, brother. If you need backup, I'm there."

"I need you here, bud. If anything happens to Ali and I... you and Jenny will be Junior's legal guardians."

Rick reached out and grasped his teammate's shoulders. "That's not gonna happen. We'll take good care of him, bud. You focus on getting Axe back."

———

Mike loaded his and Ali's suitcases into the back of his pickup while she locked the house. As he turned to see how she was doing he spotted one of Axe's favorite toys under his deck chair on the front lawn. In his mind, he could see his best friend playing on the grass with Junior.

"We're going to get him back," said Ali as she wrapped an arm around his waist.

The toot of a horn caught their attention and they saw a grey SUV pull to the curb. Through the windshield, Mike spotted TJ at the wheel and Deb in the passenger seat. The two alighted and joined them at the truck.

"You ready to roll?" asked TJ.

Mike managed a smile. "Yeah, let's do this."

"I've booked accommodation at a resort," said Deb. "The rooms are adjoining so we can coordinate the search." She gestured to the SUV. "We've got all the gear we're going to need."

"What about border control?" asked Mike.

Deb shrugged. "Taken care of."

TJ handed Mike a hand-held radio. "Crypto and frequency are loaded. We'll lead."

"OK then." Mike and Ali climbed into his truck and

reversed out onto the road where TJ and Deb were waiting in their own vehicle.

As they started down the road, Ali spoke, "Something tells me that Deborah isn't a food critique."

Mike nodded. "She's CIA."

They drove in silence before Ali spoke again. "Mike, what if this is a trap. What if Barbosa wants you to come and try to rescue Axe?"

"Deb wouldn't have agreed to help if she hadn't accounted for that risk."

"Why do you think they're keeping him alive?"

He exhaled. "I don't even want to think about that. I just want to get down there and find him."

Meanwhile, in the vehicle ahead Deb and TJ were traveling in silence, TJ behind the wheel. "Remember that time we drove down to Tijuana for the night and you…"

"Terrance, there's no need for the nostalgia. Let's keep it professional."

To TJ the comment felt like a backhand to the face. He hunched forward and concentrated on the road.

"I'm sorry," Deb said softly. "I do remember that trip. You'd just come back from Iraq. We hired that little bungalow down on the beach."

He smiled. "Yeah and that dog you fed followed us home and snored like a freight train on the porch. I didn't sleep a wink." He paused. "You always had a soft spot for strays."

From the corner of his eye, he caught the faintest hint of a smile on her lips.

"Well, today we're not hunting strays. We're hunting for Axe. Now keep your mind on the job."

"Yes, ma'am." TJ maintained his composure but inside

felt a glimmer of hope. Perhaps this trip would help them reconnect and maybe, just maybe, it could rekindle the spark that he desperately hoped was still smoldering in the depths of her heart.

Chapter Eight

Mike parked his pickup alongside TJ's SUV in the garage of the villa that Deb had booked in Cabo. He carried their bags up a short flight of stairs into an open plan living, kitchen and dining area. The ocean sparkled through the broad windows beyond a wide golden beach.

"Wow," said Mike as he dropped their bags.

Deb emerged from a door to his right and gestured to the room opposite. "Your suite is through there. We'll set up the gear in here on the dining room table."

Mike helped TJ bring some additional cases of equipment up from the SUV as Ali unpacked their bags in their room.

"Things can't be that bad if you're sharing a suite," said Mike as they retrieved the last of the equipment from the car.

TJ sighed. "Separate rooms."

By the time they'd brought all the gear up into the villa Deb had set up a laptop and laid out some of her specialist equipment. Mike identified smartphones, a small commercial drone and a bunch of other electrical devices. He shot Ali a questioning look.

"OK guys, here's the plan." Deb spun her computer so they could see a satellite image of the area on screen. "We know the phone that made the video has been active in Cabo. I've broken the town down into search sectors." She gestured to two phones that lay alongside black nylon pouches. "We'll use mustang surveillance devices to get a fix on the phone and then go from there."

"They easy to use?" asked Mike.

Deb nodded. "Yes, they're already configured. The antenna array is in the pouch; leave that in your car if you go out on foot. The basic unit has a range of about fifty yards."

"What happens after we locate the phone?" asked Ali.

"Then this goes from a find and fix operation to recovery, and that just happens to be the boy's specialty."

"Damn, straight," said Mike. "Let's get out on the ground and find this dirt bag."

"Mike, I need to cover off on a few points." Deb's tone was stern. "You need to remember your cover story. We're not down here searching for Axe. We're down here on a couple's retreat. That means we at least need to look like we're having a good time."

Ali and Mike nodded.

"And if you get compromised the drill is to head straight back to San Diego. Make sure you keep all of your personal effects on your person."

"I take it the room can't be linked to us," said TJ.

"Correct."

"Is that it?" Mike asked impatiently.

"Yes, that's all."

Mike rose and took the mustang unit from the table. "I'll set up in the truck."

Ali waited till he was gone. "Deb, Mike and I appreciate this so much. You've gone above and beyond to help us find Axe and that means the world to us."

A smile appeared on Deb's face. "We all owe a lot to that dog."

TJ clapped his hands. "Agreed, let's go out and find him."

Mike drove the pickup along a wide street bordered on both sides by small blocks of faded stucco apartments. They passed a row of dune buggies parked in front of a bar and Mike turned to his wife, who was studying the mustang device. "Anything?"

"Not yet."

He slowed the truck and indicated to turn right. "We'll box around this suburb then move to another sector."

"Mike, aren't people going to get suspicious if we keep driving around? Not as many cars on the road as I expected."

They crossed the main highway and headed down a side street. "One last circuit and then we'll find somewhere to eat." Mike scanned both sides of the street as he drove.

"Deb is very efficient."

"Yeah, brutally so."

They drove in silence.

"I think she still loves him," Ali said as they reached the end of the block.

"What makes you say that?"

"Just a feeling."

"Yeah, well according to TJ there's no feeling left. That's the problem. She's gone completely cold on him." Mike turned the truck down another street. "Still nothing?"

Ali shook her head.

Mike smacked his hands against the wheel in frustration.

She reached across and touched his shoulder. "Babe, this was never going to be easy. We're going to find him. It's just going to take a little time. How about we get something to eat and check the bar area?"

He accelerated the truck. "That's a good idea. Barbosa's guys will be neck deep in booze and broads."

"I'm not going into a strip club."

Mike managed a chuckle. "With the mustang we don't have to. Keep it in your bag and we can walk past."

They parked the truck on a side street and walked through to Cabo's primary bar and dining zone, set a street back from the marina. The low slung concrete buildings, palm trees and wide roads reminded Mike of parts of Baghdad city. Only the streets of Cabo weren't pockmarked with bullet holes and Mike didn't have his full team behind him and Axe by his side. He swallowed hard as images from the video popped into his mind. By now Axe's captors could have severely injured him, or worse.

They walked the length of the street before Ali gestured to a bright painted cantina that had a sign declaring free beer with every plate of tacos. "How about this place?"

"Yeah, why not."

They took a table on the street.

Mike watched as Ali took the mustang from her bag and checked it. He could tell by the look on her face that they'd had no luck.

She reached across the table and took his hand. "Mike, we will find him."

"Yeah, hopefully TJ and Deb are having more luck."

Chapter Nine

A little over eight miles away the other pair was conducting their sweep of the outskirts of Cabo. Under Deb's guidance TJ had configured the antenna array to maximize the mustang's collection footprint. So far, like Mike and Ali, they'd had no luck in locating the phone associated with the video of Axe.

"Damn it's dry down here," said TJ as they finished a run along a dusty road and turned back on the main route into town.

"It is a desert," said Deb, with her eyes fixed on the locator.

"Yeah, the cactuses are a dead give-away."

"Cacti, the plural is cacti."

"You sure?"

"Yes, I'm a journalist, remember."

"Really, does food critique classify as journalism?"

She glanced up at him. "In what world does it not?"

"In a world where it's a cover story and not your real job."

"I'll have you know I won an AFJ award last year for one of my articles."

TJ shot her a questioning look. "An award?"

Her eyes narrowed. "Yes, an award. Is that so surprising?"

"Not at all. I just thought someone else wrote the articles for you."

Deb turned her attention back to the mustang.

He chuckled. "You won an award for someone else's writing."

"I edited the article."

TJ slowed the SUV as they arrived at the outskirts of Cabo.

"Take the next right," said Deb.

"You're actually a talented writer. Remember when you used to keep a journal?"

"I do."

"Used to read it to me. The words were always beautiful." TJ turned the truck onto a potholed laneway that skirted the edge of the town.

She looked up and smiled. "You're a good listener."

They held the gaze for a moment before TJ turned back to the road. "Deb, what happened?"

"You stopped listening and spent all your time in the teams."

"I never stopped listening… or loving you."

"We're not doing this now, Terrance. It's too–" A loud beep emitted from the tracking device. "We've got a hit!"

TJ slowed the truck. "Where?"

Her brow furrowed as she studied the mustang. "It's behind us."

He spun the wheel and turned the SUV in a tight circle, jumping the curb.

"It's approaching the intersection ahead."

TJ eased his foot onto the accelerator and they closed the gap with the main road. Fortunately, traffic was light with only three vehicles flashing past as TJ braked at a yield sign.

"Should be the next car," said Deb.

A battered Ford Bronco appeared to their right and drove past the intersection. TJ eased them in behind and accelerated to match the speed.

"Don't get too close," ordered Deb.

"This ain't my first rodeo, sweetheart," drawled TJ in his best southern accent. "You think we should contact Mike and Ali?"

"Not yet. Let's tail the Bronco and see where it leads. Once we've got some kind of confirmation, we'll update the others."

"Right on."

As they followed the Bronco Deb took a tablet from her bag and accessed a satellite imagery app. "Not much out here other than ranches."

"They're probably holding Axe at one of Barbosa's places. He's got properties spread across Northern Mexico."

"Not out here, well at least not that we know of. I pulled the company's file on your boy. His operations and real-estate are mainly focused in Sonora and Chihuahua."

"And they haven't been hamstrung by his incarceration?"

"Not that we can see. It's business as usual."

They followed the Bronco for another five miles before it slowed and turned off the road onto a gravel track.

"Keep going," said Deb as she checked her tablet. "That road leads to a ranch in the foothills. It could be where they're keeping Axe."

TJ continued a further quarter of a mile before pulling over to the side of the road. "You want to send in the drone?"

"Good idea. There's a trail a few hundred yards up. Leads into a small valley. It should hide us from the road and the ranch."

TJ followed her directions and a moment later they were parked in a dry streambed behind a low rise.

"We've got about an hour till sunset," said TJ as he unpacked a quadcopter from its soft case. "Probably a good idea to send an update to Mike."

Deb checked her phone. "I've got no cell or sat coverage." She glanced up at the imposing mountain range to their west. "This place is a black hole."

"That's probably why they go in to Cabo." He unfolded the arms of the compact drone and placed it on the hood of the SUV.

"Have you flown one of these before?" she asked.

"You bought me one for Christmas."

"Right, that may have been my assistant?"

"The same one that wrote your award-winning article?" TJ shot her a grin and was rewarded with a faint smile. He toggled the drone's controls and sent it soaring into the sky. Deb stood next to him so she could see the screen as he orientated it toward their target.

From two miles away they could only see a cluster of buildings in a clearing. He moved the craft forward and they slowly grew in size.

A waft of Deb's fragrance hit TJ's nose. It was the same one she'd always worn; a subtle scent that reminded him of far more intimate times. He realized that they were standing shoulder to shoulder. It pained him to realize that this was the closest he'd been to his estranged wife in the last few months.

"You're kidding me?"

The angry tone of her voice snapped him back to reality. The image on the drone's screen was blurring and distorting. TJ reversed its track and the picture cleared.

"Is that normal?"

"No. It's got a three-mile range. There's definitely some kind of serious interference out here. We're going to have to get closer."

He turned his head and found himself looking directly into Deb's eyes. There was an awkward silence before he spoke. "I'll go in for a closer look."

"Not by yourself you won't."

"It would be better if you stayed here and—"

She cut him off with a withering look. "There are binoculars and radios in the truck."

TJ led Deb through thorny scrub to a position just under a mile from the ranch, where they assessed the vehicle had stopped. He lowered the backpack he'd taken from their SUV and sat under a gnarled tree.

Deb joined him and he passed her a water bottle.

"We've got about thirty minutes of light."

She took a sip and returned the bottle. TJ took a mouthful and stashed it in his pack. He pulled out the drone and set it up on a rock. "I'm going to go forward with the binoculars. If you stay here, you can use the drone for over-watch and communicate with me via radio."

The look on Deb's face told him she wasn't happy with the plan.

"We can't both go. If something happens, you need to be able to get back into cell phone range and tell Mike and Ali."

"You're right. OK, let's get this done."

TJ clipped a radio to his belt and inserted an earpiece. "Check, check," he transmitted.

"Lima Charlie," she responded over her radio as she grasped his shoulder. "Be safe."

TJ set off through the scrub at a trot. He'd cover as much ground as he could before finding a position where he could observe the ranch. With any luck he'd get eyes on the Bronco and then Axe.

The whirr of blades told him the drone was up. The noise faded as Deb sent it high to avoid detection.

"I can see you," she transmitted.

"How's the feed?"

"Grainy, but workable."

He slowed to a walk as he approached a rise that he estimated was less than four hundred yards from the ranch. Crouching low he used a bush for cover and raised his binoculars.

He spotted the Bronco parked in front of a low-slung hacienda. There were two men lifting bags from the tailgate. A third joined them to assist in carrying the supplies inside. TJ spotted a pistol on the hip of one of the men.

"You getting this?" transmitted Deb.

"Yeah, three men. At least one is armed."

"Not much of an indicator. Everyone around here carries."

TJ watched as the three men disappeared inside. He waited a few minutes and when they didn't reappear, he lowered the binoculars. "I'm going in for a better look."

"I can't get any closer. The image degrades."

"OK, just keep an eye on the front and let me know if they come out."

"Be careful."

"Yes, ma'am."

TJ slipped down the slope into the bushes that ran all the way to the edge of the clearing where the ranch was situated. He worked his way around the buildings to a weathered stockyard. Through the railings he could see chain-link fences behind the main building. They looked to him like cages. Cages like the one in the video sent to Mike.

He crouched low and worked his way along the outside of the yards. As he approached the cages, Deb transmitted a message.

"They're coming out."

TJ dropped to his stomach and slid in tight against the railing. Men's voices carried on the evening breeze as two figures appeared from the ranch house. They passed within yards of TJ as they made their way toward the pens.

He lifted his head slightly and watched them from behind the stockyard. One of the men was carrying a bloodied plastic bag. They stopped near the cage and flung something over the fence.

His heart skipped a beat when he heard a bark and a savage growl. He couldn't see the dog, but he instantly recognized the bark as Axe's. "He's here," he whispered into the radio.

"TJ, you need to get out of there." Even masked by the radio, he could hear the concern in her voice.

The men stood talking near the cages and then turned and walked back toward the hacienda. TJ lowered his head as one of them looked in his direction. He hugged the earth as the men's voices got closer.

"Don't move," transmitted Deb.

Savage barking filled the air and one of the men yelled out at the dog.

"Crawl back," said Deb.

TJ scrabbled backward along the edge of the stockyard into the cover of the scrub and rose to his knees. A glance over his shoulder confirmed that the men had moved to the edge of the yard. One of them looked to be studying the spot where TJ had been lying. As the man crouched to inspect the ground TJ backed further into the bushes, turned and ran as fast as he could.

"They're on to you," transmitted Deb. "The third guy just left the building armed with a submachine gun."

"Deb, head back to the truck. I'll meet you there."

TJ heard a shout from behind, spurring him on. He found his tracks in the sandy soil and followed them between thorny bushes and cacti. It took him less than three minutes to reach the ridge where he'd left Deb. The only sign of her was the footprints leading back toward their SUV.

"I'm at the truck," she transmitted as he jogged after her. "All three men are following you. They're about two hundred yards behind."

She must still have the drone up, he thought as he dashed through the scrub. A thorn bush snagged his arm as he brushed past it. The long spines tore into his skin, but he pressed on. Finally, with lungs heaving, he burst from the bushes onto the track where the SUV was waiting with the passenger door open. He leaped into the cab and slammed it shut as Deb gunned the engine.

The SUV took off like a startled horse, she struggled to keep it centered on the sandy track. "Close call," she said as they hit the main road and gained speed. She wore a smile as she turned to TJ. "Well done, old man."

"You did well, Mrs. Smith." He chuckled, referring to the action movie starring *Brad Pitt* and *Angelina Jolie*.

TJ checked his phone for messages as they drove back into town. He kept one eye on the wing mirror, checking for anyone following. "Mike and Ali just got back to the villa. We can update them when we arrive."

"Sounds good," replied Deb as they reached the outskirts of Cabo.

"What happened to the drone?" TJ asked.

"I sent it over the mountains. It should be running out of batteries real soon."

"Good thinking."

"Not just a pretty face."

"That's why I married you."

He glanced sideways and caught an ever so slight smile on her lips. For the first time in months, he felt a glimmer of hope that he could save his marriage.

TJ bounded up the stairs and into the living area of the rented villa where a glum-looking Mike sat at the dining room table. "I think we found him," he exclaimed.

Ali appeared from the door to their suite at the same time that Deb entered the room.

"We got a hit on the phone and tracked it to a ranch outside of town," TJ continued.

"And you saw him?" said Mike.

"No. I heard him."

Mike took his phone from his pocket and pushed it across the table to TJ. A video was playing on the screen. The SEAL Chief positioned it so he and Deb could see. It was another video of Axe being poked through a chain fence with a stick. The dog was wide-eyed with his teeth bared and his fur matted with blood.

"Does this look the same?" asked Mike.

"The cage looks like a match. We spotted three men on target. I can confirm that at least one is armed."

"We need to hit the place tonight," Mike said in earnest.

"I agree." TJ swallowed. "Our recce may have been compromised."

"They saw you?"

TJ shook his head. "No, they saw my tracks."

Mike rose and stared out the windows at the sun setting over the ocean. "If they think someone's onto them they'll move him." He turned back with a look of steely determination. "Deb, what can you do about hardware?"

"No can do. You get caught with guns in Mexico and you're screwed. You'll do five to ten in one of the worst prisons on earth." She grabbed a black pelican case from the floor and opened it. Inside was a pair of night-vision goggles and a number of innocuous looking devices that included a phone, camera and a flashlight. She took the items from the case. "The phone, camera and light contain Tasers. They will be our last resort."

Mike frowned as he grasped the camera. "We're going to go up against Barbosa's *sicarios* armed with Tasers?"

"It's doable," said TJ. "We lure them away from the ranch, grab Axe and get back across the border."

"It's our only option. You thinking a distraction?"

"Yep."

"What can we do to help?" asked Ali.

TJ nodded. "We're going to need to find a hardware store." He checked his watch. "We'll raid the ranch in the early hours of the morning."

Rick's brain throbbed as he sat on the edge of Junior's bed and attempted to distract the wailing toddler with his favorite stuffed toy. A glance at his watch confirmed it was just past midnight, meaning the toddler had been crying for two hours straight. Rick had no idea where the kid found the energy.

"Mom, mom, mom, mom," Junior chanted between sobs.

"I know bud. You're mom's going to be back soon with dad and Axe."

At the mention of the dog's name, Junior looked up at him with tear-filled eyes. "Axe," he murmured. "Where Axe?"

"He's looking after your mom and dad."

That seemed to appease the boy and he raised his arms toward Rick. The hulking SEAL picked him up and the toddler wrapped his tiny arms around his neck.

"Axe look after mom," Junior said.

Rick's heart nearly broke as he cuddled his godson. "Yes, he will."

As he comforted the boy, he reflected on the message that TJ had sent him. They'd located Axe and would be attempting a recovery within the next few hours. With any luck, Junior would be reunited with his buddy in no time.

"Oh you definitely pass the husband selection course," whispered Jenny from the doorway.

He glanced up at his fiancée. There was a smile on her face and her dark eyes shone brightly. "Huh?"

"He's asleep."

Rick turned his head slightly so he could see the boy

sleeping against his chest. "Isn't this the dad selection course?"

She stepped into the room and kissed his shaved head. "One step at a time, big guy. Have you heard from TJ?"

"Yeah, they should be back tomorrow."

"They've got Axe?"

"Not yet. In a few hours."

Rick made to lower the boy into his bed. Junior mumbled something incoherent and clung to him like a baby koala. He sighed and made himself comfortable. "I guess I'm sleeping here tonight."

Jenny kissed him again before snuggling in alongside him. "We're both sleeping here tonight."

Chapter Ten

Barbosa sat on a bench in the exercise yard with a cigarette dangling from the corner of his mouth. He gazed up at the orange sky and exhaled a cloud of smoke into the air. Cigarettes and yard time were precious commodities in prison. Commodities he purchased with wads of cash smuggled into the prison by his agents.

"Time's up," barked a gruff voice.

He glanced up at the guard. "Not yet."

"What did you say?"

"NOT YET!"

Barbosa flicked the half-smoked cigarette at the exercise yard's chain fence and fixed his eyes on the concrete wall fifty yards distant.

"On your feet!" barked the guard. "On your feet or I'll break your god damn arm."

"What's the time?" asked Barbosa as he rose.

"Time for you to go back to your cell."

"I don't think so." Barbosa fixed the man with a dark stare.

The guard's lip rose in a snarl as he raised his baton.

A massive explosion reverberated throughout the yard, and the guard's face went from rage to shock in a split second.

Barbosa smiled as the air around him exploded in a cacophony of screeching metal. He turned and saw a garbage truck slamming its way through the prison's walls and fences. It made it through two layers of barriers before it ground to a halt.

Masked men flooded in through the breach as the hiss of gas replaced the noise of the crash. Gunfire filled the air as the guards in the towers fired at the truck. A rocket streaked over the wall and detonated against the armored glass of one of the towers. Barbosa covered his nose and mouth with a hand as figures moved toward him.

"Shit!" managed the guard before an AK rattled and he was cut down in a hail of bullets.

The roar of a two-stroke engine sounded as a circular blade sliced through the fence that separated Barbosa from the assailants. In a matter of seconds the exercise yard was breached. One of the figures thrust a gas mask into his hands and he donned it.

Gunfire raged as the men led him back to the garbage truck and out through the hole it had smashed through the prison walls.

Outside a half-dozen black GMC SUVs were parked along the fence. No less than twenty gunmen were blasting away at the towers with assault rifles and rockets. The wail of a siren rang in his ears as the men bundled him into one of the vehicles. Wheels spun and they accelerated away. Safely inside, Barbosa removed his mask and tossed it onto the seat.

As he gave the prison one last glance a massive fireball

rolled into the air and the glass vibrated as the garbage truck detonated.

"A parting gift, boss," said the only other person in the SUV, the driver.

"Nice touch."

The convoy of black SUVs sped along a highway into the desert and onto a side road. They belted down a dirt track until they turned onto a small airfield. Barbosa's vehicle pulled in alongside a business jet parked under floodlights in front of a rusted hangar.

"Time to fly boss," said the driver.

One of his men opened the door and directed him into the waiting jet. As he mounted the stairs, a curvy stewardess in a tight outfit greeted him with a tumbler of his favorite whiskey on ice.

She closed the doors as the jet's turbines whined pushing them smoothly forward. He took the stewardess's cue and relaxed in a plush leather seat after downing the whiskey. The engines roared and they lurched off the tarmac and banked hard. Barely a minute had passed when the jet leveled off and the intercom buzzed.

"Sir, we've entered Mexican airspace."

Barbosa clapped his hands together. "Excellent, now bring me a phone. There's business that needs taking care of."

"Dokka dokka dokka, here comes the helicopter." Rick flew a spoonful of food around Junior's head as the boy squealed with delight, flapping his arms like a deranged bird. The boy was secured in his high chair in the kitchen of their apartment.

"Open up. Here comes the SEAL team." He shoveled the food into Junior's mouth and the toddler swallowed it in a single gulp.

"More, more," he demanded.

"OK, here it comes." Rick saw his phone flash on the counter as he reloaded the spoon. "Babe can you grab that?" he asked Jenny who was preparing dinner.

"Sure thing," she said, picking up the phone and checking the screen. "It's a message from Ernie."

Rick pushed another food-laden spoon into Junior's mouth. "What's it say?"

"Bravo has escaped and is at large." She frowned. "Who's bravo?"

Rick placed the spoon down. "Babe, you know how we discussed contingency plans?"

"Yes, is this—"

"An emergency? Yes. Can you look after Junior? I'll grab our bags and meet you at the car."

"Is Bravo the cartel guy?"

Rick nodded as he shrugged off the apron he'd been wearing to feed Junior. "Yeah, and he's escaped. We need to get Junior to World's End and wait for the others."

"World's End?" asked Jenny as she wiped the toddler's face.

"More, heli bopper," demanded Junior.

"We have to go on a trip. More heli bopper then," said Rick. He turned back to Jenny. "World's End is a safe house that TJ setup in case something like this happened. Ernie is going to meet us there."

"Do you think Barbosa is going after Mike?"

"Yeah, it makes sense. He's already got Axe."

TJ jammed the last of Deb's boxes into the back of the SUV and closed the trunk. He checked his watch. It was a little after midnight. They'd made good time in getting everything ready for the recovery op.

As the others came downstairs his phone buzzed. It was a message from Rick.

Barbosa has escaped. Taking Junior to World's End.

"Shit!"

"What's wrong?" asked Ali.

"We forget something?" said Deb.

"No, Barbosa escaped."

The look of horror on Mike's face reflected his own emotions.

"We need to roll on Axe now," he said.

TJ locked eyes with Deb who slowly shook her head. "No, it's too dangerous. You and Ali need to head back stateside and get to World's End. Ernie, Rick and the girls will meet you there."

Mike clenched his jaw. It was a look that TJ had seen before and it meant his teammate was about to defy his directions.

"I'm not going anywhere without Axe."

TJ was about to speak when Deb placed a hand on his shoulder. "Mike, you and Ali head back stateside. TJ and I will grab Axe and meet up with you there."

Ali shook her head. "No, we can't let you do that."

"You don't have a choice. You stay in Mexico and Barbosa will find you. He has no idea who I am."

"He knows TJ," said Mike.

TJ shook his head. "Deb can't go alone. Plus, we don't have kids. You and Ali have to think of Junior." TJ winked.

"I mean, imagine if Rick raised the poor kid. He wouldn't stand a chance in life."

"So that's it then," said Deb in an authoritative voice. "TJ and I will recover Axe."

Mike looked like was going to object, then his shoulders slumped. "Fine, but don't take any unnecessary risks."

TJ let out a grunt. "Oh, that's rich coming from you." He reached out and shook Mike's hand. "We'll see you guys at World's End."

Chapter Eleven

The jet's stairs lowered and Barbosa, now dressed in a well-fitted suit, descended the steps. He paused on the tarmac and took a deep breath of the night air. "Oh how I love you, Mexico!" he bellowed before striding across to the man waiting alongside a silver Mercedes G-Wagen armored SUV.

"Juan Duvan, my friend." He embraced his deputy in a bearlike hug. "Your plan was brilliant."

The mustached enforcer slapped his boss's shoulder. "It's good to have you back."

The two men entered the vehicle and it drove off the airfield followed by four SUVs.

"Where is my family?" Barbosa asked. "I thought they would be here."

"They're at the fortress. I thought they would be safer there. The Cali Cartel has been pushing the boundaries of our friendship. I'm looking forward to having you here to deal with them."

Barbosa raised a hand. "That can wait. First things first. Where is the dog?"

"He's at a facility outside Cabo."

"And the boy?"

Duvan dropped his eyes. "We are yet to locate him or his parents."

Barbosa scowled. "Bring the dog to me and find the child." He managed a faint smile as he imagined the horror on Michael Saunders' face as he watched a video of his loyal dog tearing his son's throat out. Yes, vengeance was going to be sweet and he was going to enjoy every moment of it.

TJ placed the Improvised Explosive Device he'd constructed under a shrub and toggled the switch that armed it. He'd already set two other devices and this one completed an arc a hundred yards from the western side of the ranch.

Stealing through the scrub he worked his way around to the eastern side where he'd left Deb, watching the front of the hacienda. They were dressed in a similar fashion; jeans and dark pullovers to blend with the shadows. TJ was carrying a backpack loaded with equipment. The pair also had balaclavas rolled up on their heads and night-vision devices stowed in their pockets in case the half moon disappeared behind a cloud.

"Any movement?" he asked.

"No, it's dead to the world. How did you go with the distractions?"

"They'll blow if we need them." They touched as he passed her the garage remote.

Deb closed her hand around his and gave it a gentle squeeze. "Let's do this."

TJ smiled as he moved through the darkness toward the ranch buildings. Behind him, Deb was watching the front of the main hacienda. If anyone appeared she would detonate the charges, buying him time to grab Axe and withdraw.

He paused at the edge of the yards and fished the night-vision monocular from his pocket. A quick scan of the ranch buildings confirmed it was all clear, so he moved silently toward the location where he'd seen the cages and heard Axe's bark.

As he stalked forward a strange rumbling noise came from the hacienda. He paused and then almost laughed as he realized it was someone snoring. Creeping along the side of the building he stopped a few feet short of the metal cages.

"Axe, Axe, boy."

There was a low whimper from inside and TJ spotted a shape inside the cage. He moved across, pressed his hand against the wire and was rewarded with a warm nose and wet licks.

"Axe, buddy it's you. I knew it was you." TJ felt tears forming in eyes.

The dog growled.

"Hey, buddy—"

"What the hell are you doing?" snarled an accented voice behind him. "Turn around real slow."

TJ complied and found himself staring into the barrel of a pistol.

"Don't move gringo." The man turned his head slightly and yelled out in Spanish.

There was a grunt and then yelling from inside the hacienda before a light snapped on.

"Oh shit," whispered TJ.

"Oh shit is right, gr–" The *sicario's* eyes rolled back into his head as a Taser crackled. His arms dropped to his side and he convulsed as an electrical charge coursed through his muscles.

TJ grabbed the pistol as the man dropped, revealing Deb standing behind him with the flashlight Taser in her hand. "I'm sorry, he must have snuck out of a back door."

There was another shout from inside and the sound of a weapon being cocked. TJ shrugged out of his pack and grabbed the bolt cutters inside. Slipping them onto a chain he cut through it and opened the cage.

Axe bounded from inside and jumped on the Chief, licking him. TJ snapped a lead on his collar. "Let's get you out of here."

Deb led as they dashed from the cages to the yards. TJ and Axe were halfway across when a burst of gunfire stitched the sand in front of them. He felt a bullet tug at his shirt and nick his arm as he raised the pistol.

There was an almighty flash and TJ thought he'd been shot until he realized that Deb had detonated the bombs he'd planted.

In the light from fireballs he saw two men at the front of the hacienda. Both were fixated on the blast. TJ aimed the pistol and fired. He hit one and the other beat a hasty retreat into the building.

"Come on!" yelled Deb.

TJ fired one last shot and followed her into the scrub. Axe ran by his side as she led them along a trail they'd used on the way in. Behind them a gun barked and bullets hissed over their heads.

They were halfway to the truck when TJ realized the bullet that he thought had nicked his arm had actually gone much deeper. Blood drenched his side, and he couldn't raise his arm. He felt the pistol slip from his grasp as he ran.

By the time they reached the SUV he was feeling light-headed and short of breath. Deb opened the rear door and Axe leaped into the back seat.

"Deb, you'll have to drive." He winced.

"Are you hurt?"

"I'm OK," he said climbing into the passenger seat.

She started the engine and navigated the track back to the main road. Axe shoved his head between the seats and whined softly as he pushed his head up against TJ. He patted the dog's head with his good hand as his vision spun. "Good boy."

He felt the overwhelming need to sleep as his head rocked forward against his chest.

"TJ, stay with me."

He faintly registered Deb's voice as he fought to stay awake.

"Don't you die on me you selfish bastard. Don't you leave me."

"I won't. I can't. I love you," he managed before passing out.

Chapter Twelve

Barbosa snatched a heavy tumbler from the desk in his study and flung it against the wall. It hit the rosewood paneling with a dull thud leaving a dent and dropped onto the thick carpet. "How the hell did they find the dog?" he screamed at Duvan.

"I don't know, boss. They must have had help," his head of security responded tentatively.

"Of course they had help."

"My men hit one of them. There was a blood trail leading to a vehicle. I warned out our people all the way up Baja. We've got our police running checkpoints and people checking every hospital, doctor's surgery and pharmacy. They won't get far, we'll find them."

"You better." Barbosa took a new glass from a tray on his desk, added ice cubes and poured himself a new drink. "I want you to triple the bounty on Petty Officer Saunders and his family. Spread the word."

"You still want him alive?"

"Yes, I want him alive. He's going to pay for everything he's done to me. Now, get out there and find that dog."

Duvan left the office with his phone pressed to his ear. He had contacts in almost every US agency with interests in Mexico. If the dog was still on the peninsular his people would find out where he was being hidden.

———

TJ's eyes snapped open and he reached for a pistol that he wasn't wearing. As his eyes slowly focused he realized he was lying in a bed in a well-lit room with a white ceiling. He winced as he sat up so he could take in his surroundings. There was a single window with a blind and a door opposite the bed.

As the activities of the night before came flooding back he went to raise his arm and found there was a tube running into the back of his hand. A sideways glance confirmed that someone had put an IV line in. A check of the opposite arm also revealed that his gunshot wound had been dressed.

There was a soft whine from beyond the edge of the bed and a wet nose gently nudged his hand. "Hey, Axe," he croaked.

The door to the room opened and he turned his head to see Deb carrying in a tray.

She placed it on a side table and sat on the edge of the bed. "You gave us quite the scare last night."

"Where are we?"

"An Agency safe house."

"Did you stitch me up?"

"It was the least I could do. I let you down last night. That first guy should never have gotten past me."

TJ reached over and placed his hand on top of hers. "You were amazing." He tipped his head toward his arm. "You saved my life."

She turned her hand and interlocked their fingers. "There was a moment there when I thought I'd lost you." A tear formed in her eye. "I realized I couldn't bear the idea of you not being in my life."

They locked eyes and TJ squeezed her hand. She edged forward on the bed and he leaned forward until their lips touched. His heart raced as the kiss gained in intensity. Deb's hands ran up his torso to his face and he took his good arm around her back and pulled her closer.

Axe whined from the side of the bed and made a beeline for the door. As TJ and Deb broke for air they spotted his tail disappearing out of the room and laughed. Then he kissed his wife again. This time her hands wandered south and for the first time in almost a year he felt her touch.

He winced and lifted his injured arm to pull the needle and IV line from his hand.

"You lost a lot of blood," Deb whispered.

"I almost lost a hell of a lot more." He managed to slip his hand under her shirt and release her bra.

"This isn't going to fix everything."

"No, but it's a good start, right?"

Rick skidded a Polaris ATV to a halt behind a rocky outcrop. Leaping from the seat he grabbed his M4 carbine and headed up a goat trail. It was a chilly winter's day, but he still managed to work up a sweat under his body armor. By the time he crested the ridge he was breathing hard.

Pausing for a moment he took in the sweeping vista of desert that reached out to the horizon. World's End was a rural property that belonged to a close friend of TJ's. The owner, a former Agency man, had added some significant security improvements. One of those was the reason Rick was out patrolling the perimeter.

He made his way along the ridgeline to what looked like a cell phone tower. The structure was actually an array of sophisticated sensors that included thermal cameras, vibration monitoring gear and communications intercept modules. It was part of the broader security network that piped data to the ranch house, three miles away. This particular tower had recently reported an error message.

As he approached the tower he spotted the problem. An access panel had popped open in the wind and birds had built a nest inside. "Sorry guys." He stripped the debris from the hole and closed it.

A noise to the west caught his ear as he patrolled back to the ATV. He took binoculars from a pouch on his rig and lifted them to his eyes. Far out over the desert he spotted a cloud of dust.

"Alpha, this is Bravo, I've got a vehicle inbound," he transmitted over his radio.

"Alpha here," responded Jenny. "That call sign is friendly. Get your ass back to the ranch, lunch is on."

Rick scrambled down to the ATV and gunned it across the desert. Insects bounced off his goggles and slapped into his face as he approached the ranch house. Parking, he joined Jenny and Junior under the sweeping verandahs of the renovated hacienda.

His fiancée was dressed in combat pants and T-shirt with a pistol on one hip and the toddler on the other.

"Looks good on you," he said, slipping out of his armor.

"Pistol or the kid?"

He kissed her on the cheek. "Both."

Behind them a glass door slid open. "Mike and Ali are inbound," reported Ernie as he entered.

"Any news from TJ and Deb?" asked Jenny.

"Yeah, they're in a secure location with Axe and will extract tonight. They should be here in the morning."

A horn sounded as the approaching vehicle passed the outer fence of the home block and drove up the gravel drive.

"Axe, Axe, Axe," chanted Junior as he recognized his father's pickup. It pulled in alongside the ATV. The doors swung open and Mike and Ali appeared. Ali made straight for the porch with her arms extended.

Jenny had already lowered the toddler and he took off across the grass still chanting the dog's name.

Ali swept him into her arms and hugged him tight as the others gathered around. "My darling boy. I missed you so much."

"Mom, where Axe?" he asked.

"He'll be back tomorrow," said Mike as he joined them. "Guys, thanks so much for looking after him." He hugged Jenny and shook hands with Rick and Ernie.

"It was our pleasure," said Jenny. "Come inside, we've got lunch on the table."

Mike updated the rest of the team on TJ and Deb's success in locating and extracting Axe.

"So, all going well, they should be here tomorrow?" asked Ernie.

"Yeah," said Mike. "Now, what do we know about Barbosa?"

"His people smashed their way into a maximum security prison, snatched him and detonated a massive IED to cover

94

their tracks. They killed a half-dozen guards and at least thirty other prisoners."

"Brutal," said Rick.

"Axe's abduction had to be part of this plan," said Mike.

"I agree," said Ernie. "And so do the FBI. They want to put you all in witness protection."

Mike shook his head. "No. We're not spending our lives running and hiding. Once TJ and Axe are back we need to find a way to neutralize Barbosa. We need to go on the offensive."

The ring tone of Duvan's phone sent an involuntary shiver down his spine. He glanced at the screen, hoping it wasn't another call from Barbosa demanding an update on the search for the dog. So far his people had failed to locate any trace of the animal or the people who had snatched it.

This time it wasn't Barbosa.

He answered. "Tell me good news."

"I've got a tip off," his source replied. "The people you're looking for might be in a safe house near Los Barriles." He rattled off an address.

"Where did you get the information? Is it good?"

"It's from the inside. It's good."

"It better be." Duvan terminated the call and dialed Barbosa. The cartel kingpin answered immediately.

"Have you found them?"

"I've got a lead on a safe house in Los Barriles."

"Good, get as many men together as you can. I want the dog alive. Kill everyone else."

Chapter Thirteen

TJ managed to slide his wounded arm into his shirt and fasten the buttons with one hand. Then he left the room where he'd been resting and explored the CIA safe house where he, Deb and Axe were laying low.

He found Deb in the kitchen making dinner with Axe by her side. She was still dressed in the tactical outfit she'd been wearing the night before. "Hey gorgeous."

She turned and smiled. "Coffee?"

"Yes please."

"How are you feeling?" she asked as TJ sat at the kitchen table. Axe moved to his side and placed his chin on his thigh.

He stroked the dog's head. "Pretty good, thanks to you."

"Terrance…"

He winced at the sound of his given name, she only used it when she was about to deliver a lecture.

"What happened between us doesn't fix the problem." She poured him a cup of black coffee from a percolator on the bench. Turning she registered the pained look on his face. "Don't get me wrong, it was wonderful. It's just…" She passed him the mug.

"Yeah, I know. But I also want you to know that I'm willing to do whatever it takes to rekindle what we had."

"It's not that simple."

Axe growled.

"Clearly someone disagrees."

She smiled faintly. "Well, he is the matchmaker."

Axe growled again and headed out into the hall toward the front door. TJ noticed that his hackles were raised. "Have you got a weapon?"

"In the basement. What's up?"

He rose from the chair. "Probably nothing, but–"

Axe's bark was one that TJ had heard before. The dog was alerting them to an impending threat. "Show me the basement, now!"

Deb dashed into the corridor and he followed her through a side door and downstairs. "Axe, come," he ordered as they descended into a small room filled with shelves of supplies. Deb gripped the corner of a rack of boxes and slid it sideways revealing a selection of weapons and equipment. TJ grabbed an ammunition-laden vest, wounded arm forgotten, dropped it over his head and fastened it around his torso. Axe stood at the top of the stairs, guarding the door.

Deb opened another hidden panel exposing a row of CCTV screens. She studied them intently as TJ geared up. "I can see two vehicles."

He joined her at the screens. The safe house was located a short distance from the beach and backed on to scrubby dunes. One of the cameras showed two pickups parked among the dunes. Gunmen were clustered around them, their attention focused toward the safe house.

"Why are they waiting?" asked Deb.

"They're waiting for more of their buddies. Once they have the numbers, they'll storm the joint. We need to get out of here and fast."

"If it weren't for Axe they'd have got the jump on us." Deb took a vest and submachine gun from the rack. "What's the plan?"

TJ loaded and cocked a rifle. "They'll have the road blocked. The beach is our best option."

"Good idea." She gestured to the screen where another vehicle had joined the others. "More of their friends."

TJ grabbed a backpack filled with ammunition and slung it over his shoulder. "I'm on point. You got the keys?"

She nodded. "What about Axe?"

"He knows his way around a gunfight, right bud."

The dog gave an excited bark.

TJ led them out of the basement and through the house to the porch that overlooked the beach. Their SUV was parked to one side. TJ figured they could get to it unobserved then make their escape. He checked Deb and Axe were close behind and descended the porch to the sandy lawn. Crouching at the corner of the house he peered past the SUV to where the cameras had revealed the massing gunmen.

"Cover me," he whispered to Deb.

"No." She placed a hand on his shoulder. "I'll drive. You shoot."

The stubborn look on her face told him not to argue. "OK, use the key not the remote, it will flash and draw attention."

She nodded and stole forward to the side of the SUV. As she inserted the key in the driver's door he moved forward to the passenger side. Opening the door he gestured for Axe to jump inside.

As the dog leaped in a burst of gunfire sounded from behind and bullets smacked into the side of the house. TJ spun and spotted figures approaching from the road. He returned fire as Deb started the SUV, and then clambered in.

Axe barked excitedly as they rocketed across the lawn, smashing through a white picket fence before bouncing over low dunes onto the beach.

The SUV fishtailed wildly as Deb turned and ran it parallel to the dark blue ocean.

"Steady on," grunted TJ as he climbed between the seats into the rear. Axe licked his face as he clambered into the cargo area. "Thanks, bud."

"What are you doing?" asked Deb as he found the lever to release the trunk door.

"Preparing for company." He braced his legs either side of the opening and aimed his rifle down the beach. They were a few hundred yards from the house when the first of the *sicario* trucks appeared.

"Right on cue," said TJ as he squeezed off a volley of shots.

"How far do you want me to go?" yelled Deb.

"Get us back on the road as soon as you can."

"OK."

TJ fired again as three pickups accelerated after them. Sitting on massive tires with powerful engines the trucks ate up the distance between them. He spotted muzzle flashes from above the cabins as men in the beds of the trucks fired. A bullet shattered a side window, spraying him with glass as he fired back.

"You OK?" he yelled between shots.

"Yeah, there's a track ahead. I'm getting us out of here."

He fired again and a jet of steam burst from the hood of one of the pickups. As he switched aim to another vehicle he was thrown sideways as Deb sent the SUV careening off the beach. Shrubs lashed the sides of the car as they blasted along a narrow track. Tires squealed as they turned abruptly onto tarmac.

"You OK back there?" yelled Deb.

TJ glanced over his shoulder and saw Axe calmly watching him with his tongue lolling and ears flapping in the wind.

"Yeah I'm good," he said, replacing an empty magazine with a fresh one from his vest.

"I'm going to contact my people and arrange an extraction," said Deb.

"Good idea." TJ turned his attention back to the road as they accelerated around a sweeping bend. "We need to stay off the main highway."

He fished his phone from his pocket and checked the screen, no reception. "Typical," he mumbled.

"How's the arm?" asked Deb as they turned onto a dirt track.

With the adrenaline of the gunfight and escape, he'd completely forgotten the injury. A glance confirmed that the bandage was intact and the wound wasn't weeping. "All good. Your stitches are holding."

"Who would have thought? I mean considering how crappy my sewing is. Remember that time in New Zealand when I tried to fix your pants?"

"How could I forget? I inadvertently exposed myself to a table of old ladies." He glanced over his shoulder and caught her looking at him in the mirror. Her eyes were shining and there were smile lines around them. She held his gaze for a moment before returning her attention to the road.

TJ turned to check if they were still being followed but couldn't see anything through the dust cloud trailing behind them. Despite their precarious situation Deb was softening, he was sure of it.

———

As TJ and Deb made their way north toward the border, Mike was pacing the living room at World's End. He hadn't been able to get through on the Chief's number. With every passing minute he was getting more and more worried. It was unlike TJ not to check in or make timings. Something had definitely happened.

He heard footsteps on the terracotta tiled floor and turned to see Ali approaching with a concerned look. "Any news?" she asked.

"No, nothing."

She wrapped an arm around his waist as Ernie and Rick appeared.

"You guys get through to TJ?" Mike asked.

"Negative," answered Rick.

"Well, let's hope that Deb can get her people to help out."

"Not sure how a fine dining magazine is going to help get them out of Mexico?" Rick said, with a confused look.

"She's Agency," said Mike.

"No shit!"

"I did not see that coming," said Ernie. "Although it does explain a few things."

"And it means she can get them out, easy. TJ and Axe are in good hands," said Rick.

"Unless something's happened to them. What if Barbosa's men caught up with them? We're literally sitting on our hands here," said Mike.

Rick grasped his shoulder. "Bud, you need to think of your family. If you go charging down to Mexico, they could lose both you and Axe."

"And that's exactly what Barbosa wants," said Ernie. "Let's give TJ and Deb a little more time. I've got a feeling they're going to come through with the goods."

"We've got a tail!" yelled TJ over the wind rushing into the SUV as it tore along a desert road. He'd spotted the outline of a pickup in the thick dust they were throwing up behind them.

Bullets cracked past his head, tearing into the roof of the SUV and exiting through the windshield. His heart lurched as he turned and saw holes directly in front of the driver. "Deb!" he yelled.

Her head bobbed back into view. "I'm good. I'm good." More gunfire sounded and the SUV shuddered. "Can you do something about that?"

TJ blasted into the dust with his rifle. Remembering the backpack he dug into it and found a grenade. Tearing the pin free, he popped the handle and counted down.

"Five, four, three, two." He lobbed the grenade into the dust. "One, zero."

The bomb detonated with an angry flash in the dust. He raised his rifle and waited for the truck to reappear. Seconds passed without it emerging. "That'll slow them down."

"We've got a town coming up," said Deb.

As she slowed a loud scraping noise filled the cabin. "Ah, TJ. I think they hit something vital."

The noise increased in intensity as she limped the SUV into a dusty town and pulled in alongside a row of dune buggies and pickups parked in front of a bar.

"We need some new wheels," said TJ as he jumped from the back of the SUV. Axe joined him as he eyeballed the vehicles. He strode across to a pickup truck with huge tires and exposed shock absorbers. It had tools strapped to the hood, spare wheels in the back and on the cab roof. "This will do nicely." He opened the driver's side door and saw the keys in the ignition. "Deb, we've got a new ride." He tossed his backpack into the cab and whistled for Axe to join him.

"You couldn't find something less obtrusive?"

"We need to get off the roads and head through the desert."

TJ turned over the engine, and the high-performance V8 rumbled to life. As he backed the truck out onto the street a figure appeared from the doorway of the bar.

"Hey, what the hell are you doing?"

Deb waved at the man as they roared down the road. "You're crazy, TJ." She laughed as they raced out of town.

"Crazy is going to keep us alive." TJ glanced in the mirror and spotted one of the pickups that had chased them from the safe house. "We've got company. Time to head into the desert."

He bounced the off-roader over a ditch, pointed the nose north and gunned the engine. The custom machine spat sand from all four tires as it blasted across the desert, leaving their pursuers in its wake. Deb wrapped her arms around Axe as they bounced over rocks, smashed through shrubs and launched over dunes.

After five minutes of bashing their way through scrub TJ reached a track heading roughly north. A further hour and they'd progressed a significant distance up the Baja peninsula toward the US border, winding their way through rocky outcrops and clusters of cacti, as TJ now knew was the plural for the prickly plants.

"It's got a rugged, uncompromising beauty that takes your breath away," said Deb as they crested a low ridge, revealing a broad basin. The sun was low in the sky, and the shadows cast by the rocks and bushes looked like fingers clutching at the shifting sands.

"Sure does," he replied as they descended a rutted section of trail.

As they drove across the valley floor the big V8 missed a beat and spluttered. TJ frowned as he studied the instrument panel. The temperature needle wasn't in the red, oil pressure was good and the fuel gauge hadn't moved from full. He tapped the glass with his finger and the needle immediately dropped to zero. It had been stuck on full. "Son of a bitch."

"How far are we from the border?" asked Deb as the engine died.

"At least twenty miles."

"We could walk out."

He shook his head. "Not at night in this terrain. We need to get away from the truck and hole up. Your people can extract us in the morning, right?"

Deb hauled her satellite phone from her bag and checked the screen. "Yeah, as soon as we go firm I'll update our position."

Axe whined, and TJ jumped from the cab to let him

out. He immediately relieved himself on a cactus before patrolling the area around the truck while TJ and Deb gathered their gear.

"They'll expect us to keep heading toward the border." He gestured to a rocky outcrop a mile or so to the east. "There might be a cave up there."

TJ found a bottle of water in the truck and stashed it in his pack. Then he led the threesome across the desert floor as the sun was setting behind them. In the distance he heard the snarl of engines, possibly dirt bikes. Their escape into the desert had bought them time, but it hadn't shaken Barbosa's men. They were still being hunted.

TJ crouched alongside a boulder with his rifle in hand, staring out at the pinpricks of light flashing in the darkness. Vehicles had been crisscrossing the desert all night, searching. He flexed his hand to get the blood moving through his wounded arm. The temperature had dropped with the sun causing it to ache. Satisfied that none of the lights were heading in their direction he turned and made his way back to the cave where Axe and Deb were camped.

"Are they still looking?" asked Deb from the darkness as he ducked inside.

"Yeah, but north like we thought." He gave Axe a pat and sat beside him.

"You mean like 'you' thought," she said. "You've done a pretty good job keeping us out of trouble."

"It's been a team effort."

"Just like staying warm. Come sit next to me."

TJ shuffled across till he was alongside his wife.

"It's so cold," Deb said as she snuggled in close,

lowering her head to his chest. On her opposite side Axe lay facing the opening of the cave.

TJ sat silently, enjoying the intimacy.

"I'm sorry," said Deb.

"Sorry for what?"

"Putting my career before you. Not taking the time to build on our relationship."

TJ sighed. "I'm sorry for the same things. I'm sorry I put the team first when it should have been you."

Deb chuckled. "That was never going to happen. I married a man dedicated to serving his country and his teammates. I guess I just hoped that I would be a part of that team."

He slid his injured arm around behind her back and pulled her closer. "Deborah Lines, you are my team."

There was a soft growl from Axe.

"Oh, you too bud."

The dog rose from where he was sitting next to Deb and growled again.

"What is it," she whispered.

"Could be a coyote. I'll check it out."

She kissed his cheek. "Be careful."

TJ rose and followed Axe outside. The dog disappeared into the gloom as he emerged from the cluster of boulders and scanned the horizon. He could see more now that sunrise was less than an hour away. As he patrolled the ridgeline he was on edge, as every cactus resembled a human figure, a potential threat.

Confident that the coast was clear he made his way back. Deb had already updated the Agency on their location and extraction was due at daybreak. He checked his watch. That was only thirty minutes away. He needed to get Deb up and moving.

He was halfway back to the cave when a voice stopped him dead in his tracks.

"*Manos arriba, gringo.*"

He slowly raised his hands in the air, letting his rifle hang from its sling. A gunman stepped out from behind a boulder a few feet distant, aiming a submachine gun at TJ's face.

"You're going to make me rich *essé*," the man said.

A terrifying snarl sounded from atop the rock next to the *sicario*. The man turned and saw Axe poised to strike.

TJ snatched up his rifle and swung it in a tight arc, connecting with the *sicario's* temple. As the man dropped he sprayed a burst into the distance, gunshots echoing across the valley. A split second later shouting sounded from the west.

"Axe, come." TJ sprinted for the cave. Skidding into the opening, he grabbed his bag. "Deb, we've got to go."

"Are you OK?" she asked.

"Yeah, but we're about to have company."

This time it was Axe who took point, leading them down a boulder-strewn slope that offered good cover. TJ let Deb and the dog push ahead, turning every few seconds to check for pursuers.

He paused behind a boulder, and in the soft glow of dawn, he spotted a swarm of men scrambling over the hill where they'd camped. Lining one up he squeezed off a shot and was rewarded with a cry of pain.

Muzzles flashed on the hillside and bullets ricocheted off rocks as he turned and sprinted after Deb and Axe. He jinked from side to side to throw off the aim of the attackers. Breathing hard he skirted a cluster of cacti and nearly ran into his wife crouched behind bushes with Axe. "Deb, we need to keep moving."

She grabbed his leg. "Get down."

He knelt alongside them. "What's up?"

"Look." She pointed at a rise to the east, the direction they were traveling.

TJ spotted figures silhouetted by the orange sunrise. He counted at least six gunmen blocking their escape route.

Gunfire sounded from behind, and he spun, readying his rifle. The bullets struck to his right, cutting off another avenue of escape.

"What are we going to do?" whispered Deb, her weapon held ready.

TJ could hear the fear in her voice. "We go north as fast as we can, stay low." He grabbed her hand, and they ran together with Axe following behind. Shouting filled the air as the *sicarios* gave chase. Bullets hissed past and ricocheted off rocks as they weaved between cacti, bushes and rocks.

TJ knew it was only a matter of time before a bullet hit one of them or the men caught up. Strangely he wasn't afraid. He was overcome with a feeling of rage. Finally, he'd found a connection with his wife, and now these men were going to take that from him. "Keep going," he yelled as he spun and fired on the closest of the gunmen.

As they dove for cover he fired again and again, cutting down two pursuers. He tossed his two remaining grenades, turned, and sprinted after the others. A quick calculation in his head confirmed he was down to the last of his ammunition.

He found Deb and Axe hunkered down in a cluster of rocks. Deb greeted him with a grim look, her submachine gun held ready. "They've cut us completely off."

TJ took up a firing position behind a rock. He felt the reassuring presence of Axe and glanced down at the loyal dog. He and Deb could surrender, but he owed it to Axe to keep him out of the hands of Barbosa.

Bullets ricocheted off the rocks as the cartel goons moved in.

"TJ, you can't let him fall into their hands again. We won't get a second chance at finding him," Deb said softly as she stroked the dog's ears.

"I know." He choked back tears.

TJ could see a line of men approaching from the east. A glance around confirmed that the others were holding firm.

"It's now or never," he said softly.

Deb's eyes were rimmed with tears. "I can't watch."

"He won't feel a thing."

At that moment a ripping sound filled the air. It was a noise that TJ knew from his time in Afghanistan... it was salvation.

A black helicopter thundered overhead, spewing rounds from the machine guns poking from each side of its fuselage. It cut a lap above them before touching down in a clearing a hundred yards distant.

"Go, go, go!" bellowed TJ as he shepherded them toward the helicopter.

The door gunners waved them forward between bursts of fire aimed at the fleeing cartel gunmen. Deb clambered into the chopper followed by Axe who turned to make sure that TJ was close behind. He jumped in and slumped into one of the webbing seats as they lifted off. Locking eyes with Deb, he shook his head. "That was a close call," he mouthed.

"You were amazing," she replied.

"No, you were beyond amazing."

She smiled and took a headset from one of the loadmasters. She listened for a moment then leaned forward so he could hear her. "We're being transferred to a CIA helicopter in Hermosillo. They'll take all three of us up to World's End."

He gave her thumbs up as she slid into the seat next to him. On his opposite side Axe sat looking out over the desert with his ears flapping in the wind.

"How's your arm?" she asked.

He grimaced. "I think I may have finally torn your stitches."

She placed her hand on his thigh and gave it a squeeze. "As soon as we land I'll have a look at it."

Chapter Fourteen

Rick paused from where he was cleaning his rifle and watched as a white unmarked helicopter thundered in, cutting a tight lap around the World's End hacienda as the pilot surveyed potential landing zones. The lush green lawn at the back of the residence, beyond the swimming pool, was the selected spot.

Rotor wash lashed the vines that grew over the rear of the adobe building as he joined Mike, Jenny, Ernie and Ali, holding Junior, who were waiting to see who alighted.

The doors of the unmarked chopper slid back and a blur of brown and black dashed from the idling aircraft.

Axe rounded the pool at high speed and made a beeline for the group.

Mike dropped to a knee. "Axe, Axe, boy."

Rick choked back tears as his buddy wrapped his arms around the excited animal.

"Axe," cried out Junior as he recognized the dog. Ali lowered him to the ground and the toddler hugged his best friend as Axe licked his face.

"That's so sweet," said Jenny as she took his hand.

Ali bent and gave the ecstatic hound a quick once-over. "Looks like he's in good health."

Rick glanced back at the helicopter and spotted TJ and Deb. TJ's wife had her arm around his waist, and he looked to be wearing a sling.

Mike met them at the edge of the pool. "I can't thank you guys enough." He hugged Deb before turning to TJ. "What happened? You OK?"

The craggy SEAL nodded. "Yeah, Deb took good care of me."

Behind them, the helicopter's blades thundered as it took off into the setting sun.

"Let's get everyone inside," said Ali as she scooped Junior from the ground. "Dinner's on the table and I've been saving a huge bone for Axe."

As they moved inside Rick noticed that TJ and Deb hung back. He nudged Mike and tipped his head in the direction of the couple. "Looks like Axe has done it again."

Mike nodded. "Cupid in a fur coat. Let's leave them to it."

TJ gazed out over the desert with one arm around his wife, the other hitched in a sling. "Deb, what you did for the team and me—"

She cut him off by grasping his face and kissing him. "You were amazing out there," she said breathlessly when they broke. "That was the Terrance I fell in love with; a man of action, a man of passion and power. That's the man I wanted to live the rest of my life with."

"I've always been that man, Deb."

"Yes, but not for me. I never get to see you. Both of us have been married to our jobs."

"For me, that's going to change."

"How? It's always been the SEALs first."

TJ shook his head. "Mike's a dad now, Ernie has his family, and it won't be long till Rick and Jenny get started. It's about time we all slowed down a little. I've requested the team be moved over to training."

Deb's eyes narrowed. "Training? You'll be bored in a week."

"Maybe." He leaned in and kissed her again. "But that's a risk I'm willing to take."

The kissed lingered for a moment before she pulled away. "I've got a better idea. How about I get the team attached to the Agency's South American Special Activities Division?"

"You can do that?"

Deb nuzzled in against his neck. "Of course I can. I'm the Regional Director."

"When did that happen?"

"About a month ago." She took his hand.

"Is this because of your journalism award?"

Deb laughed. "Yeah, that's it." She led him toward the ranch house, from which the smell of roasted meat was wafting. "Now come on, I'm starving."

Hours later, with Junior in bed, the team sat on the porch of the ranch house drinking whiskey and smoking cigars. In the distance a coyote let out a mournful series of yips, triggering a low growl from Axe.

Mike ruffled the dog's ears. "Easy boy."

TJ took a puff of his Cuban and exhaled a ring of smoke into the air. "You know Barbosa isn't going to let up."

The others were silent.

"Till that guy's neutralized, Mike, Ali, Junior and Axe are always going to be in danger."

Rick nodded. "Always looking over your shoulder. You can't live like that, brother."

"So what are we going to do about it?" asked Ernie.

Mike sighed. "What can we do about it other than hiding? Barbosa's resources are next level. He's surrounded by guards, constantly moves and we can't hit him with an airstrike." He turned to Deb. "Can we?"

"No." She sipped from her whiskey. "However, a few years back someone took down a cartel operation in Chihuahua. High speed, clandestine type stuff. They cut down *sicarios*, corrupt cops and mercenaries like they were nothing."

"Agency guys?" asked Ernie.

"No, there were a bunch of corrupt CIA contractors involved. They didn't fare much better."

"And you think these guys could take down Barbosa?" asked TJ.

"Oh, there's no doubt about it."

"But, they're mercenaries and mercenaries cost money, right?" said Jenny.

"Something tells me these guys aren't motivated by money. Plus, if rumors are true, and they usually are, I used to work with one of them."

"Ex-CIA?" asked Mike.

"Correct. Vance was one of the Agency's best till he was presumed killed with his partner in a botched operation in the UAE. However, his partner turned up in Afghanistan three years later, wounded but alive."

"And you think they're running some kind of vigilante group taking down bad guys?" asked Rick.

"Knowing Vance, that's exactly what they're doing."

Mike locked eyes with his wife.

"We're running out of options," Ali said quietly.

"Can you get in contact with them?" he asked Deb.

"I think I know a way."

TJ rested his hand on Mike's shoulder. "OK, let's make it happen then."

Chapter Fifteen

TJ turned a battered Ford Explorer onto an equally neglected airstrip and brought it to a halt alongside the rusted hulk of an ancient Anderson aircraft hangar. "This is it."

Deb, dressed in tan cargo pants and a loose fitting green shirt checked her phone. "In position and on time."

"You really think these people can help us?" asked TJ as he un-holstered his pistol and confirmed there was a round chambered.

"I hope so, for Ali and Junior's sake. Jumping from safe house to safe house is no way to raise a kid."

TJ nodded as he took a handheld radio from the belt under his jacket and spoke into it. "Team, how we looking?"

"In position," reported Rick.

"Same here," said Ernie.

"Ready to rock," added Mike.

All three men were positioned around the airfield and armed with marksman rifles. They had infiltrated overnight to provide protection to Deb and TJ as they met with the shadowy organization she'd contacted through a former CIA operative.

"Team, I apologize for my tardiness," a strange voice emitted from the radio. "I'll be with you in a moment."

TJ turned to his wife. "That's an encrypted radio."

"And now it's compromised." Deb stepped out of the vehicle and scanned the horizon. It was less than an hour after sunrise and the sky was clear. "I can't see anything."

As TJ joined her they heard a sound like ruffling sheets above them. They glanced up and spotted a figure descending under a black parachute.

"These guys are pretty switched," said TJ.

The rest of the team was silent now that their radio network had been compromised. They watched as the parachutist cut tight turns, descending toward them. Then, a dozen feet above the ground, they flared and executed a controlled landing. The operative bundled the chute, removed their helmet and used it to weight the nylon fabric.

The operative rose and TJ saw it was a man. His guess was mid-thirties with a trim waist and broad shoulders. As he approached, he got a good look at his face. He had intelligent brown eyes, a strong stubble-covered jaw and a crooked nose, suggesting he wasn't one to shy away from a fight.

The man's equipment spoke to the sophistication of his unit. He wore a lightweight parachute harness the likes of which TJ had never seen before. It was the type of rig that the SEALs dreamed of using instead of the bulky setups the Navy supplied. Interestingly, he could see no evidence of a weapon or communications equipment.

The man extended a hand to Deb. "Hi, name's Bishop."

She shook it. "I'm Deb, this is TJ."

Bishop shook his hand with a firm grip. TJ thought he identified a slight twang to the man's accent, but he couldn't place it.

"Your buddies in overwatch. They going to join the party?"

Deb smiled thinly. "I like them where they are."

He shrugged. "Fair enough. Just so you know, my people have got them covered from above."

TJ glanced skyward; he could see no sign of an aircraft or drone.

"So, tell me everything you know about Barbosa," said Bishop.

Deb reached into her pocket and removed a flash drive, which she handed to the man. "This is everything that the Agency knows."

"But, you can't get to him?"

"I wouldn't be talking to you if we could."

Bishop nodded. "We'll look into it, but I can't make any promises."

"Got a lot on your plate?"

"You know how it is. No shortage of work."

"There's one piece of information that won't be on the stick," said Mike as he rounded the SUV dressed in head to toe camouflage and carrying a sniper rifle. "The Butcher has a clown phobia."

The clandestine operative smirked. "I might have to crack out my Pennywise costume," he said, referring to the clown character from Stephen King's, *IT*. "You must be Mike."

Mike slung his weapon and shook the man's hand. "Yeah, pleased to meet you, Bishop. Look, I've got a favor to ask."

"You want in on the mission, right?"

"Yeah."

"Figures, if some guy was trying to kill my family and friends I'd want to be the one taking him down. Look, I can't promise anything, but I will run it past my people."

"Appreciated."

"OK, is there anything else?"

Deb's eyes narrowed. "How's Vance doing?"

"Not bad for a dead man. He sends his regards. Allegedly, he thinks very highly of you, or this meeting would never have happened." Bishop took a phone from his pocket and tapped the screen. "I guess this is where people would expect a speech about this meeting never happening." He slipped the device back into his pocket. "But, we're all professionals, so it's not necessary." He turned to Mike. "I'll be in touch."

TJ sensed warmth in the man's smile as he shook hands with each of them.

"A pleasure." Bishop turned and nodded toward the end of the runway. "That'll be my ride."

TJ turned and spotted a speck on the horizon. It rapidly grew into an aircraft that touched down in a cloud of dust. A parachute flared from behind and the sleek white business jet slowed with a roar of engines.

"Catch you on the flip side."

TJ shook his head as the man jogged across to the jet as a set of stairs dropped. He stepped inside and it closed. Then there was an almighty roar and the aircraft blasted off the dirt strip with twin jets of flame spewing from its turbines. Within seconds it was airborne and streaking away.

"God damn," said TJ.

"Impressive," added Mike as he watched it disappear.

"Did you see any markings on that jet?" asked Deb.

"No, but I think we're dealing with a very capable organization," said TJ as they moved away from Mike toward the SUV.

"The Agency made the exact same assessment."

TJ slipped an arm around his wife's slender waist. "So, tell me more about this Vance character."

She turned and kissed him on the cheek. "Don't be jealous, it was a purely professional relationship. We worked together on one of my first field operations."

"And he thinks highly of you?" TJ mimicked Bishop's accent.

She laughed. "Darling, he was compromised and abducted. I managed to tail his kidnappers and a paramilitary team recovered him before they could work him over."

"You saved his life."

"I guess you could say that."

"My wife the super agent." He kissed her on the lips.

"Hey, get a room guys," Rick's voice hissed over the radio.

Deb grabbed TJ's handset from his belt. "Need I remind you that these means have been compromised."

"I think we all know who's going to get compromised," replied Rick.

Mike laughed as he joined them.

Deb shook her head as they climbed into the SUV. "Your teammates."

"Correction, our," said TJ. "They're your teammates too."

Barbosa sipped his coffee as he listened to one of his lieutenants outline the reason that drug production from one of his labs had slumped. Allegedly, the farmers he forced to supply the cocaine had chosen to grow food, limiting their output of coca leaves. "How long has this been going on?" he asked as a servant brought in his breakfast of poached eggs on salmon, drizzled with pesto.

"About three months," replied his man. "There has been a drought—"

He cut the lieutenant off with a wave of his hand as he stuffed a laden fork into his mouth. "There are no excuses," he mumbled.

The man nodded.

He swallowed. "Take two families." He paused to sip his coffee. "And kill them."

"Even the children?"

Barbosa stared at him over his cup. "Children, grandparents, chickens, cats, dogs. Kill them all. Set an example for the others."

"Yes, boss."

"Actually, forget it. I'll look after it myself." He wiped his chin with a crisp white napkin. "Is my car ready?"

"Yes, boss," one of the bodyguards loitering in the background replied.

Barbosa downed his coffee and left the dining room. His wife farewelled him in the foyer of their luxurious home and he strolled out to where a convoy of three armored SUVs were parked.

His head of security, Duvan, was waiting at the middle vehicle with the door open. "I've got good news, boss."

Barbosa climbed into the rear of the SUV. Duvan slammed the heavy door and rode shotgun in the front passenger seat.

"One of our people got some red hot intel on the SEAL and the dog."

"Have they found them?"

"No, but we know they're going to be attending a wedding in Washington state, tomorrow, along with all their friends."

The cartel boss gazed out of the window as the vehicle started moving. "Get as many shooters as you can. Make it a bloodbath. Kill everyone and everything."

"I'll make the arrangements."

As the convoy left the heavily guarded estate Barbosa took a tablet from a seat pocket to check his sharemarket portfolio. His forehead wrinkled into a frown as the device refused to link to the cellular network. He tried for a minute and then tossed it on the leather seat in disgust. Again, he tried on his phone where he encountered the same problem. "What the hell is wrong with the network?"

"Towers must be down," said Duvan.

Barbosa scowled as his car slowed and came to a halt. "What now?"

Duvan spoke into a radio before reporting to his boss. "There's a clown on the road."

"A what?"

"Some guy dressed as a clown. He's holding a red balloon."

"What the hell?"

"Yeah, weird shit. Stay here, boss, I'm going to check it out." Duvan opened the door of the armored SUV.

"No—"

Duvan let out a grunt and toppled over.

"No, no, no." Barbosa struggled through to the front seat and grabbed the door, pulling it closed. "Get us out of here!" he screamed at the driver.

There was a blinding flash. He glanced through the windshield and saw the lead vehicle engulfed in flames. "Go!"

The armored SUV rocked as another blast crippled the vehicle behind it. Then the driver angled the wheel and stomped the accelerator to the floor. Barbosa was flung sideways as the truck bounced over a curb and stalled.

"Get it going!"

His man struggled with the ignition, but the truck refused to start.

"Pump the gas."

Still, the engine refused to catch.

He caught a glimpse of movement through the side window. A figure was approaching through the smoke from the burning vehicles. As they got closer, he saw it was an armed man wearing a clown mask.

Barbosa fumbled for his pistol as the grinning clown approached the window. He winced as a gloved hand slapped a written card up against the glass. His blood ran cold as he read the neatly printed words.

This is for Axe, Ali and Junior. But... mostly Axe.

The figure tore off his mask and Barbosa found himself face to face with Petty Officer Mike Saunders, the man whose life he had pledged to destroy. Mike glared at him with grim determination and waved with a gloved hand.

There was a loud thump from under the SUV. Barbosa turned to the driver who was still trying to start the engine. "We need to get out." He crawled through to the back seat with his pistol in hand and fumbled with the door latch. It wouldn't open.

He turned back to the window where the message was stuck to the glass. There was no sign of the SEAL.

Barbosa, *The Butcher*, had a split second of remorse as the floor beneath him was super heated to a half-million degrees by a thermal charge. Then, he felt nothing as he was instantly incinerated.

A few hundred yards away Mike stood with a second clown, watching the vehicle burn. The other clown tore off his mask, revealing a crooked nose and brown eyes.

"Job done," said Bishop.

Mike felt like a massive weight had been lifted from his shoulders. With Barbosa dead his family would no longer live in fear. The cartel boss's reign of terror was finally over.

"Thank you," said Mike.

"No dramas. Dealing with scum like him is what PRIMAL does," replied Bishop.

"PRIMAL, hey. Well it's good to know that someone out there is willing to take out the trash."

Bishop laughed. "That's one way of putting it. Now, we need to get ourselves to a wedding."

"Does Rick look nervous?" TJ whispered to his wife. They sat with fifty other people on benches under the sweeping boughs of the forest that surrounded his family cabin. A string quartet played softly in the background as Rick and his best man, Mike, waited for the arrival of his bride.

She nudged him gently. "I do remember you being pretty nervous when we got married."

"That's because your father was carrying a gun."

Deb chuckled. "Terrance, he was a cop."

"That made it worse."

She took his hand a squeezed it gently. "Well, you didn't look nervous yesterday."

As a precursor to Rick and Jenny's wedding the two of them had held a small commitment ceremony for just the teammates and their friends. It was TJ's idea to reaffirm their vows and there hadn't been a dry eye in the cabin when they'd finished.

"Oh my god, that's so cute," gushed Deb.

TJ turned his head and saw Junior, dressed in a miniature tuxedo, leading Axe along the red carpet that split the rows of people sitting on benches. The little boy was grinning as he clutched the collar of the former Military Working Dog. He noted that Junior wasn't actually leading the dog. It was Axe who was guiding the toddler down the aisle. He smiled. Axe was wearing a bowtie on his collar.

The two of them stopped alongside Rick where he was standing with Mike. The groom wore a grin wider than the Golden Gate Bridge.

"This is to die for," whispered Deb.

TJ turned and kissed her on the cheek as the string quartet increased in tempo and volume. All eyes were drawn to the aisle as Jenny appeared from behind a massive sequoia tree. She was radiant in an elegant ivory off-the-shoulder dress with intricate beading around the bust. Her father wore a stern expression as he escorted his only daughter down the aisle.

TJ felt a tear forming in his eye. Then, he nearly laughed as he realized the quartet was playing a string rendition of Beyonce's *Single Ladies*. "Last man down," he whispered as the bride joined the groom.

An hour later, with the bridal party having photos taken in the woods, TJ found himself at the outside bar drinking champagne with Deb, Ernie and his wife, Maria.

"Wasn't that a beautiful ceremony," said Maria.

"Stunning," agreed Deb. "And it went flawlessly."

As small talk continued, TJ spotted a familiar face among the guests milling among the wine barrels and rough-hewn benches being used to hold food and drinks. The man from the meeting in Mexico, Bishop, was talking with a group of Jenny's friends from New York. "Deb, look who it is."

His wife didn't miss a beat. "Oh, how lovely he could make it." She excused herself from the group and they moved toward Bishop.

The clandestine operative broke from his own conversation and met them half way.

"What a surprise to see you here," said Deb as she offered her hand.

Bishop shook both their hands. "Deborah, you look stunning. TJ, good to see you again. I apologize for the intrusion, but our people got wind of a plan for Barbosa's people to target the wedding. We wanted to make sure that nothing happened."

TJ's eyes scanned the surrounding forest and he contemplated making a beeline for the gun cabinet in the cabin.

"There's no need to be alarmed," he added. "The key threats have been neutralized. We just wanted to make sure there were no residual elements in play." Bishop took a flash drive from his suit and handed it to Deb. "There are details of his known associates included with his jackpot card."

Deb shook Bishop's hand. "We owe you guys a debt of gratitude. Tell Vance he will always have a friend inside the Agency."

"Appreciated."

"Who invited this clown?" Mike appeared with Ali, Junior and Axe. The SEAL and his wife both wore carefree smiles. Junior greeted Deb and TJ with squeals of delight as Deb lifted him from the ground.

"Hello handsome," she said as Mike shook hands with Bishop and introduced him to Ali.

The boy wrapped his arms around her neck. "Hello Aunty Deb."

TJ bent and stroked Axe's ears as his wife cuddled the toddler. He rose when a waiter brought a tray of drinks to the group and Ernie and his wife joined them. Behind them he spotted Rick and Jenny. Accepting a flute of champagne he waited for the couple to arrive. "Ladies and gentlemen, a toast."

The others followed suit.

"To the newlyweds."

They echoed the toast and everyone sipped. Then Rick raised his own glass. "Most importantly, to Axe. The best damn dog I've ever met."

"Axe, Axe, Axe," chanted Junior as the adults raised their glasses then drank.

"So, Mike," said Bishop. "Any chance Axe has a girlfriend? Because if he ever sires pups I want one."

"Me too," said Ernie.

"Amen to that," said Rick.

"I don't think you'd have any problems homing them," said Jenny. "We'd take two."

Mike glanced down at Axe. "Seems only fair that we find him a lady, I mean, he helped me get mine."

"Me too," said Rick.

"Same here," said TJ as he leaned across and kissed his wife on the cheek.

"What do you think, bud?" Mike asked his loyal friend. "You ready to be a dad?"

Axe let out a bark, rose up on his rear legs and placed his paws on the barrel.

"Looks like he's interested," Ali said with a laugh. "And I just happen to know a very available and very beautiful Alsatian."

"Hang on," said Ernie. "Does this mean we're going to have to run a canine girlfriend selection course?"

More by Jack Silkstone

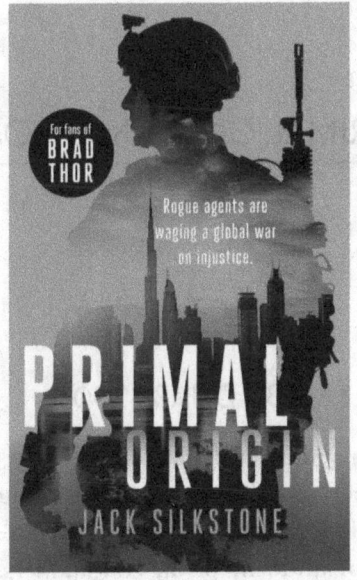

vinci-books.com/primal-origin

They are the unseen guardians, the avengers of the innocent, the destroyers of evil.

In a world where governments fail, PRIMAL delivers justice with a dose of fury. This is the first book in the PRIMAL Origin thriller series, a page-turning, gripping tale of vigilante justice against evil.

Turn the page for a free preview…

PRIMAL Origin: Chapter One

ABU DHABI, 2004

The US Embassy in Abu Dhabi didn't impress Vance. Like so many other buildings in the Emirates, it was a monstrosity of steel and glass, chilled to almost arctic temperatures by an army of air conditioners. A CIA paramilitary officer, the solidly built African American wasn't bothered by the heat of the Arabian Gulf. He'd been in the country for over a month and was fully acclimatized. So much so, he was shivering as he waited for an audience with the ambassador.

"They always have it up too high," the secretary said.

Vance attempted a smile. "Yeah, it keeps the penguins working."

The pretty blonde laughed and returned her attention to her computer.

He scanned the room again. It was lavishly furnished, some new vogue designer's attempt to give it some warmth. The marble floor was laid with ornamental Persian rugs.

Expensive paintings graced the walls on either side of a pair of solid mahogany doors that barred entry into the ambassador's office. It was nothing like the rough compound he'd called home for the past five weeks.

Vance and his offsider, a former Marine known as Ice, were working with a World Health Organization team in an industrial sector of the desert city. They had established a health clinic to support thousands of the city's impoverished workers. In a US Government–sponsored initiative, the team was currently checking for any signs of a superflu pandemic.

From Vance's perspective, the WHO team was providing cover for the CIA to track down a terrorist group. In the last month, a spate of suicide attacks had rocked the Gulf States, targeting Western expatriates and government officials. CIA analysts had assessed that the attacks were linked to the recent US invasion of Iraq. However, one of the suicide bombers had been identified as Bangladeshi, recruited from the UAE's immigrant workforce.

Vance and Ice had been sent to Abu Dhabi to track down the recruiters and follow the link back to the terrorist command structure. So far the few leads they'd uncovered had been dead ends. Despite this, Vance's experience and gut instinct told him they were hunting in the right place.

A buzzer sounded on the secretary's desk. "Sir, the ambassador will see you now." She rose and walked across to open the solid wooden doors.

Vance extracted his muscular frame from the sofa and followed her into the ambassador's office. The opulence of the waiting area was magnified tenfold in the huge room. Tall, blast-proof, tinted windows reduced the sun's glare but allowed a sweeping view of the malls, hotels, and high-rises that had sprouted from the oil-rich sands of Abu Dhabi.

This was the office of a man at home with wealth and power.

Howard D. Beecroft sat behind his antique desk and examined Vance with a critical eye. He noted with scorn the dusty boots, grubby khaki cargo pants, and faded blue shirt. His gaze lingered on the weathered features of the CIA veteran.

"So this is the renegade running black ops in my Emirates," Beecroft said.

"I'm sorry: black ops?" Vance returned the scornful gaze, equally unimpressed with the bureaucrat.

Beecroft sported a portly frame and ruddy complexion, the result of years on the cocktail circuit. "Yes, the CIA didn't seek my approval for your little mission." His chins wobbled as he spoke.

"Last time I checked, the CIA didn't work for the State Department."

Beecroft tipped back in his soft leather chair. His belly strained against a tailored waistcoat under a dark blue suit. Vance almost expected to see a gold chain disappearing into the vest pocket.

"I don't think you understand, Mr...." The ambassador paused, unable to recall Vance's surname. "I don't think you understand just how important the Emirates is to America. The lifeblood of our nation flows through this relationship and it is my job to ensure that nothing damages that. That no obstacles block the flow. Obstacles like you."

Vance's brow furrowed. "Don't get me wrong, I understand the situation. But what I don't get is how a discreet CIA operation could be considered an obstacle."

"Discreet? Is that what you think your little mission is?" Beecroft selected a manila folder from a pile on his desk. "If it is so discreet, then explain to me why the head of the

Special Tasks Branch is sending me reports warning that you are, in fact, the next target for the very terrorists you're supposed to be hunting?"

He threw the folder on the desk. "Your operation has the potential to severely embarrass my standing with the Emir. I can only hope that he isn't aware of your activities already."

Vance stepped forward to pick up the folder. It contained a single-page police report. He skimmed it and dropped it back on the desk. "How the hell did they find out we're here?"

"Evidently your World Health Organization cover isn't as good as you think."

"I call bullshit on that, Mr. Ambassador."

"How it happened doesn't matter." Beecroft waved his finger as he spoke. "The simple fact is you've been compromised and now you're out. I'm sure you can hunt terrorists in Iraq or Afghanistan. My aide has arranged tickets for you and the—"

"Get the WHO team out, but I'm staying."

Beecroft pushed back his chair and struggled to remove his corpulent frame from its clutches. He finally got to his feet, drawing himself up to his full five feet nine inches. "You will do no such thing. This is my post and I will—"

"You will sit the fuck down, Ambassador!" Vance growled from a height advantage of almost six inches.

Beecroft shrunk like a deflated balloon, dropping back into his chair.

"The only way we could have been compromised is through this office."

The ambassador opened his mouth to object but Vance cut him off again. "Now. You're probably not harboring Bin

Laden and co, so my guess is you blabbed to one of your buddies at poker."

Beecroft opened his mouth to protest, but thought better of it.

"Now usually I would get very, very upset about that, but this time I'm gonna let it slide. What I won't be doing is getting on any airplane."

The ambassador's face turned a brighter shade of red. "You will get on that plane. Otherwise I will submit a report to Washington."

Vance smiled. "You go right ahead and do that, Mr. Ambassador. By the time your report gets read and someone takes notice, my job here will be done. So you just get back to protecting the flow of oil and I'll get back to tracking down our nation's enemies." He turned and walked toward the door.

"This will be the end of you, Vance. I'll make sure of that."

"Take your best shot, Mr. Ambassador. Better men have tried."

Ice was waiting in the parking lot when Vance exited the building. He wore similar clothes to the senior CIA operative: tan cargo pants and a loose-fitting shirt. The former recon Marine was chatting with a member of the Embassy's Marine security detail. The guard was a big man, at least six feet, but the paramilitary operative towered over him. With short blond hair, a square jaw, and the build of an NFL quarterback, Ice was a formidable-looking individual.

Spotting Vance, he shook hands with the Marine and

walked back to their Toyota Land Cruiser, starting the engine.

Neither man said a word as Ice drove them from the embassy, until the battered four-wheel drive had merged into Abu Dhabi's hectic traffic.

"Where we heading, boss?" Ice asked.

"Find a place to park. I need to make a few calls."

"That bad?"

"Yes and no." Vance gave him a rundown on the conversation with the ambassador. "If the police report is accurate, we've been compromised and now the hunter has become the hunted," he concluded.

"There's more good in this than bad," Ice said after a moment.

"How's that, big man?"

"The way I see it, the ambassador's done us a favor. Now we know for sure that this terrorist group has links to the Emirates government. We just need to flush them out."

Vance looked sideways. "Ice, you're nuts. I tell you a bunch of jihadist douche bags are gonna try and blow us to hell and you think it's a good thing." He shook his head and laughed.

The corner of Ice's mouth turned up in a slight smile. His eyes never left the packed highway.

Vance continued. "Only problem is that pompous cock-sucker has given us the boot. It won't take Langley long to follow that up and shit-can us."

"Means we need to move fast."

"Yep. First things first, we get the Doc and his crew out." Vance pulled out his phone and scrolled through the contacts, looking for the physician in charge of the WHO team. "After that I'll arrange a meeting with Tariq and find out how Special Tasks were alerted to the attack. You check if the gear has arrived."

Ice pulled into the parking lot of one of Abu Dhabi's shopping malls and slotted the four-wheel drive into a free spot. Vance was already talking to the head of the WHO team. Ice jumped out of the vehicle and dialed the FedEx Custom Critical depot to check if the extra equipment he'd ordered from Langley had arrived. With a direct threat to the team, he'd be happier packing a little extra heat.

PRIMAL Origin: Chapter Two

An hour later, Vance was waiting in an emergency fire escape at the Al Wahda shopping mall. A symbol of the Gulf city's progress, the mall was a sprawling complex of over 120 high-end retail outlets. Vance hated it, all sparkling marble and glass, built by unskilled immigrant labor with petrodollars. Like so many things in the Middle East, the glamor was a thin veil. In the staircase, behind the scenes, the flaking paint and exposed wiring told another story.

Vance checked his phone. His contact was late. A moment later it buzzed and a message displayed on the screen:

Contact is moving toward your loc

Ice was watching the approaches to the emergency exit. Despite his stature, the CIA operative had an uncanny knack for remaining out of sight. Vance felt comfortable knowing the big man had his back.

The door swung open and a man in a dark suit barged

in. He gave Vance a cursory nod and scanned the stairwell. Vance lifted his arms, allowing himself to be patted down. Security procedures complete, the man exited through the same door. A few seconds later Vance's contact entered.

"It is good to see you again, Vance." Tariq Ahmed, the head of Abu Dhabi's Police Special Tasks Branch, was every inch the charming gentleman, his slim frame clad in an immaculately tailored suit, dark hair slicked back, beard and mustache trimmed to perfection.

"You too, Tariq. Been a while."

Prior to assuming his current mantle, Tariq had been an intelligence officer in the UAE Army. He had worked with Vance in Afghanistan.

Tariq's face remained impassive as he spoke. "I wish we were meeting under better circumstances." He folded his arms across his chest. "You should have listened to Mr. Beecroft."

"What the hell, Tariq? Goddamn tangos want to take down my team and you're going to let a pen pusher like Beecroft stop me from taking them out?"

"Mr. Beecroft is a powerful man. If you value your career, I would suggest you follow his direction."

"My career? Tariq, I've been in this business for long enough and one thing I've learned is that Langley doesn't give a shit about me. No, this is personal now. I want these jihadi fucks head's on a slab!"

Tariq raised an eyebrow at the tirade. "As do I, Vance, and I assure you we have the situation well in hand."

"Yeah, twelve dead in three months. Looks like you've got it well in hand." Vance gave a hard stare. "Does it bother you that someone in your government is sponsoring the murder of innocent civilians?"

Tariq's eyes narrowed. "How do you know that?"

"I didn't, but I suspected as much. Now you've all but confirmed it."

"There is more to this than you think, my friend."

"Clearly. That's why you're meeting me in a goddamn stairwell."

"Leave this to my people; the CIA has no role to play here. This is an Emirates problem and we will resolve it. You should focus on Iraq."

It was Vance's turn to fold his arms. "No role? You feed us some crap about a terrorist group targeting my team and then you tell me I don't have a role to play in it. Screw you, Tariq, I thought we were friends."

"We are, and that is why you were warned."

"Don't think I'm not appreciative, buddy, but you need to give me a whole lot more than that. Who's your source?"

"I cannot reveal that."

"Then give me some details. Who's leading the attack? When's it planned for? What type of attack? A suicide bomber? A car bomb?"

"The attack was to occur in the next twenty-four hours; a VBIED into the medical clinic. That is all I know."

Vance didn't believe for one second that the well-groomed Arab was sharing everything.

"Listen, trust me when I say this." Tariq's gaze softened slightly. "There is nothing more the CIA can do here. Your embassy has booked a flight for you tonight. You would be well advised to take it."

There was silence as the two men stared at each other.

"Maybe you're right," Vance said.

Tariq smiled halfheartedly. "You're making the right decision, my friend. Have a safe trip and perhaps we will meet again under better circumstances." With that, the head of Special Tasks Branch disappeared through the door.

Vance waited a few seconds before moving down the stairs to the underground parking level. He exited the stairwell and walked across to where the Land Cruiser was parked.

A few minutes later Ice joined him. "Only the one guy with him, Vance. He's trying to keep it discreet."

"Yeah, could mean he's being watched."

"Do you trust him?"

Vance shook his head. "I'm not sure, but I'd wager he knows a shitload more than he's telling."

"Any more intel on the threat?"

"Yeah. Car bomb into the compound. Next twenty-four hours."

"Think it's reliable?"

"Tariq and I worked together in the 'Ghan. He pulled my nuts out of the fire a couple of times. If it wasn't for him, I would've ended my run holding my own head on YouTube." Vance opened his car door. "So yeah, I think it's good. I've just got the feeling he's still hiding something from us."

They climbed into the Land Cruiser and Ice started the engine. "From what I've read in *Forbes*, his father's a very powerful man."

"Damn straight he is. The emir's chief security advisor, and in his spare time he runs a multi-billion dollar logistics company."

"So if Tariq's hiding something, it's gotta be big." The tires of the four-wheel drive screeched on the polished concrete as Ice nosed it toward the exit.

"You're right. If we uncover a terrorist cell operating inside the UAE government, it would be a major embarrassment. That's why he wants the CIA out. Not that it would matter. That prick Beecroft would sacrifice his own mother to keep the oil flowing."

"The terrorists could have a royal link," added Ice.

"True. Some rich, bored asshole getting his kicks out of playing jihad. Whoever it is, he fucked up though."

"How so?"

"By trying to kill us."

"So what's the plan from here?" Ice asked as he lowered the window and paid the foreign worker who manned the parking booth.

"We get our gear from the depot and stake out the clinic. Jihad jerk-off's posse are bound to do one last recon. We'll leave the lights on and maybe they'll still be keen to join our little party."

PRIMAL Origin: Chapter Three

Despite being the home of over five thousand immigrant workers, Abu Dhabi's Musaffah industrial complex was deathly quiet under the dark shroud of a moonless night. Vance had parked the Land Cruiser in a side alley around the corner from the WHO clinic, hidden from view but still positioned to allow quick access to the street. On the seat next to him was a laptop, the screen displaying images beamed from two cameras hidden on the high walls of the WHO compound. One showed a view down the street to the front, the other covered the narrow alley that ran behind.

Vance panned a camera to the construction site opposite the clinic. The street lighting was dim and the green hue of the infrared camera made the half-built sheds look like the skeleton of a prehistoric beast. A cat, hunting rats in the rubble of the building site, leaped from a Dumpster, landing gracefully alongside a pile of builder's waste.

"Here, kitty, kitty," Ice's voice came through over the radio.

Vance watched the cat arch its back and streak away into the darkness. He panned the camera back over the area. "Damn, Ice, I can't see you. I'm looking straight at that heap of crap you're under."

"I'm a trash ninja," quipped Ice. His tone changed. "Vehicle approaching."

A battered pickup approached down the street, its headlights off.

Ice gripped his silenced Beretta tightly and flicked the safety off. "This looks suspect."

Vance panned the camera toward the threat.

The pickup coasted down the street, slowing in front of the clinic, and came to a halt directly opposite Ice. It paused, then veered toward him, bouncing over the low curb.

"Shit," whispered Vance as it stopped mere feet from his hidden partner. The doors opened and two men wearing dark clothes jumped down from the cab.

Ice slid one hand under his body, ready to spring from his hiding spot.

"These guys look like some sort of amateur recon team," whispered Vance as he watched them through the camera.

Ice clicked his transmit button once in response. One of the men was standing almost directly on top of him. The one closest to Ice moved around the vehicle into the shadows cast by the lights of the compound. The truck now separated them from Ice.

The two men just stood in the shadows watching the street. Minutes passed before Ice whispered, "What's the plan? Take one down and get the other to talk?"

"Negative. Something's not right, just sit tight."

A moment later the two men began moving around the

construction site. They talked in hushed voices and used a flashlight to probe the piles of building materials.

"I think we've got ourselves some lowbrow thieves," whispered Ice.

"Roger."

The scavengers attempted to load a heavy metal beam into the back of their pickup. A set of headlights flashed down the road and they dropped it with a crash. Vance smirked as the would-be thieves clambered to find a hiding spot behind their truck. He focused the camera on the approaching vehicle. It was a Mercedes, not unusual for Abu Dhabi.

"You got eyes on?" he asked over the radio.

"Yes," Ice whispered.

The saloon slowed almost to a halt as it passed by. On his screen Vance could make out a faint glow on the passenger-side window. It took him a second to realize what it was; a video camera.

"These are our guys, Ice. Tag 'em."

As the Mercedes accelerated from the clinic, Ice broke cover. The pile of trash materialized into a man wielding a gun. The two would-be thieves, startled, ran yelling into the building site, tripping over the debris.

Ice aimed the Tippmann paintball marker at the Mercedes and squeezed the trigger. The ball left the barrel with a snort and slapped the rear right wheel. It burst, spraying a clear liquid across the side of the car.

"That's a hit," reported Ice.

"Nice shot. Now let's find out where these clowns are hanging out."

PRIMAL Origin: Chapter Four

Six hundred miles above Abu Dhabi, a satellite adjusted its sensor array on an isolated bandwidth of radiation. Within a few seconds it had located a target. A complex algorithm converted the information into a military grid reference and relayed it to the requesting entity.

Back on the ground, Ice had joined Vance in the Land Cruiser. He was still wearing his combat rig, a balaclava rolled up on top of his head.

"You smell like shit!" Vance said as he hunched over his laptop.

"Next time I'll sit in the car while you crawl in the trash."

"No thanks, bud. I'm getting too old for all that sneaky peeky crap."

"Have we got a track?"

"I've got the grid. Plotting it now." Vance opened the mapping program and entered the grid reference from the satellite. "Target's about four miles away, still in the industrial sector. Looks like a medium-size warehouse with a high brick wall." Vance handed the laptop to Ice and started the car. "You're the shooter, Ice. How we gonna crack this one?"

Ice had planned hundreds of raids in Afghanistan and Iraq. "I think we're going to have to get in close."

It took a little over ten minutes to cover the distance to the warehouse. They parked a few hundred yards out and advanced on foot. Both men were equipped similarly: combat body armor worn over their shirts and Nomex bala-clavas covering their faces. They carried suppressed weapons; the last thing they wanted was to alert the local authorities. Ice favored a UMP45 submachine gun and Vance a M4 CQBR carbine.

They hugged the shadows as they moved stealthily to the twelve-foot brick wall surrounding the target warehouse. The only entry point was a well-lit steel sliding gate.

Crouched in a ditch beside the wall, Ice pulled a compact screen from his vest. He uncoiled a flexible camera and plugged it into the device. With Vance scanning for threats, he stood and held the setup at arm's length, allowing the camera to see over the wall. He panned it back and forth, recording imagery.

Seconds later he was back in the ditch reviewing the footage with Vance. "There's the Mercedes. No sign of anyone; they might be all in bed."

"I doubt it. They're probably going over their recon footage."

"We should drop in for a critique."

"Any wire on that wall?" Vance peered closer at the screen.

"Negative. Your balls are safe."

Ice packed the camera away and followed Vance over the wall. He slid across the top of the brickwork and dropped onto the gravel parking lot in front of the warehouse. The Mercedes was parked in front of a roller door. A smaller entrance was off to the right and Ice guessed it led into the building's office.

They followed the wall around, avoiding the light from above the front gate. As they neared the entrance, Ice signaled to halt. He left Vance in cover and crawled to the office door. The tiny camera snaked under the rubber seal at the bottom, giving an insect's view inside.

It was unoccupied with a single light illuminating a desk and chairs. An AK assault rifle was on the desk; Ice could make out the distinctive stock, along with a pair of night-vision goggles and a laptop. He relayed his findings to Vance over the radio.

"It's your call, big man."

"Silent entry. I'll lead." Ice turned the door handle. It wasn't locked. With a click, the door popped inward. He pushed it open and crept inside.

He froze. At the other side of the room, standing in the next doorway was a young man in white robes. They stared at each other for a moment, until the youth dove for the AK on the table. Ice's UMP spat twice and the heavy slugs tore into the target's torso. The body smashed into the table with a crash.

"Shit," whispered Vance as he stepped into the office.

Ice was already moving. He stepped around the body and through the next door. Bright overhead lighting caused him to squint as he entered the open space of the warehouse. He sensed a tall figure lurch at him from the side. A blow knocked the UMP from his hands and it dropped onto its sling. He reacted by swinging his right arm in an arc, pushing his assailant's pistol up against the wall.

He turned his face away as a blow impacted on the side

of his head. His vision flashed red and he staggered. With his right arm pinning the pistol to the wall, he spun his left elbow, driving it into the face of the attacker. There was a crunch and a crash as a man fell backward against the sheet-metal wall. Before the body hit the floor, Ice swung his UMP up, and fired a burst into its chest.

In the few seconds it had taken Ice to dispatch his assailant, Vance had calmly stepped past. Deeper into the warehouse another man in white raised a pistol. Vance shot him twice in the face, his suppressed carbine making a sharp, slapping noise. The 5.56mm bullets punched through soft bone and tissue. The man dropped like a puppet with its strings cut.

The warehouse was new, shelves on the walls still empty. A white minivan was parked facing him. Vance noted it was sitting low on its axles. The smell of fuel hung in the air.

Faintly, above the hum of the fluorescent lighting, Vance could hear chanting. It was coming from the van. He padded cautiously toward the vehicle, his weapon tight against his shoulder. As he approached the rear with a series of shuffling side steps, the red dot of his Aimpoint sight came to rest on the forehead of another young man. This one was sitting in the back of the van, eyes wide, chanting softly to himself.

"Ice, we've got a big fucking problem."

"Moving."

In the back of the van, the teenager was sitting on a layer of small bricks wrapped in wax paper. He was clutching what looked like a slot-car controller.

"Release-activated detonator," Ice stated from behind Vance, "and probably at least half a ton of C4."

"I've seen this before," said Vance. "You see how he's clean-shaven, head and all. I've seen this before in Yemen.

He's been purified for the big bang. Poor bastard's well and truly been brainwashed."

"None of them are Arabs, except maybe the big one by the door. At a guess I'd say this guy's Pakistani."

Vance lowered his carbine and pulled off his balaclava. "It's OK, son. You don't need to do this. Just hand me the clacker, alright?" He reached out with one hand.

The boy's eyes grew even wider and his chanting more earnest. He threw his hands in the air with a scream, "*ALLAHU AKBA—*"

There was a thud as Ice shot him cleanly through the head. The body fell backward, blood splashing across the bricks of C4.

Both of them waited for the flash that would send them to the afterlife.

"How the fuck are we still alive?" Vance asked in a low voice.

Ice climbed into the van and picked up the remote from where it had fallen. He traced the cable, lifting blocks of explosives to reveal the detonation system. The wire ran into a simple circuit with a battery and a cell phone. Electric cables like the arms of an octopus snaked out to half a dozen detonators embedded in the C4. Ice cut the circuit board free and held it up to the light. "The remote's a dummy. Whoever set this up didn't trust his bomber. The phone's the only way to activate it."

Ice tore the phone from the circuit and passed it to Vance. It began vibrating and a buzzing filled the air. Vance spun around, eyes searching the room. He sprinted across to the man who had attacked Ice earlier.

Unlike the three youths, this guy was big, at least six feet, with a heavy build. His face was dark and angular with a hawk-like nose. Ice's bullets had torn into his chest and he was lying in a growing pool of thick blood, a cell phone clutched in his hand. Vance crouched over him and held out the other buzzing phone.

"Looking for this, motherfucker?"

The man coughed. Blood ran out of his mouth and down his neck. He wasn't going to last much longer.

"Who do you work for?" Vance growled as he grabbed the Arab by his shoulders and effortlessly propped him against the wall. If he could stop the lungs from filling, maybe he could keep him alive a little longer.

"You—you should have gone home, CIA pig," coughed the man. "You're a dead man now."

"You and your buddies had your chance, pal. Now how about you tell me who you're working for and maybe I won't go after your family."

"Maybe... you should... ask your friend, Tariq." With that, the man's head slumped against his chest.

Vance checked for a pulse.

"Dead?" yelled Ice from the next room.

"Yep." Vance scrolled through the man's phone. It only had the one number saved in the contacts. He emptied the corpse's pockets and pulled out a wallet. "You're not gonna believe it, Ice. He's Emirates Police. One Yussuf Bishara."

"That makes sense. Check this out."

Vance walked into the office where Ice was standing over the desk, scrolling through a presentation on the laptop.

"Pretty damn slick," observed Vance. The slides showed a detailed plan for the attack on the WHO clinic, complete with surveillance photos.

"Whoever put this together was a pro: definitely military, cops, or intel," agreed Ice.

Vance stared at the screen for a few seconds, then

looked up. "Grab the laptop. I'll take some photos and we'll get the hell out of here. I want to have another chat with our man Tariq."

**Grab your copy...
vinci-books.com/primal-origin**

About the Author

Jack Silkstone grew up on a steady diet of Tom Clancy, James Bond, Jason Bourne, Commando comics, and the original first-person shooters, Wolfenstein and Doom. His background includes a career in military intelligence and special operations, working alongside some of the world's most elite units. His love of action-adventure stories, his military background, and his real-world experiences combined to inspire the no-holds-barred PRIMAL series.